TILLY & THE UNREFORMED RAKE

SHADOWS AND SILK, BOOK 8

SOFIE DARLING

USA TODAY BESTSELLING AUTHOR

1

BRIGHTON, ENGLAND, NOVEMBER 1835

To someone from the outside looking at her life, Tilly might not have given the appearance of a person who had come up in the world.

She was a lady's maid, and there were folk who looked down their snooty noses at lesser personages than themselves.

Lesser personages.

A phrase she'd picked up over these last nine years.

Not from her employer, Lady Percival, of course.

Naw, Isabel was the best of the best.

Isabel didn't see Tilly as a *lesser personage.*

Now, other personages out in the world—the East End world Tilly had sprung from—would've taken the opposite point of view.

They would say she'd come up.

They might even say she'd acquired some airs about her along the way, too.

And they'd be right—on the first count, anyway.

As far as the second opinion went, some folk never liked other folk *getting above themselves*.

Tilly didn't pay a lick of mind to those folk.

If she'd not gotten above herself and stayed where she'd come from, she would still be face down in the muck, now wouldn't she?

The minute Isabel had taken her hand nine years ago and said, "*Is this the life you want?*" and when she'd said further, "*Come with me,*" Tilly had—and she'd never looked back.

Not even once.

"Is it a supper party you're attending tonight?" Tilly had Isabel's long sable hair in hand, and she needed to know before she began styling it. "A little early in the day for a supper party, ain't it?"

Isabel's striking green eyes met hers in the mirror. "*Sí.* A dear old friend of the duke's invited us to view his gardens before the other guests arrive." A little smile curved her mouth. "We dare not miss."

By *the duke*, Isabel meant the Duke of Arundel.

Her husband Lord Percival's pa.

That was how much Tilly had come up in the world— lady's maid to a duke's daughter-in-law.

As for Isabel's hair, Tilly knew exactly how Isabel liked it styled for a supper party—severely parted in the middle, smoothed back, and arranged in a chignon at the nape of her neck.

Most ladies couldn't carry off that hairstyle.

But Isabel could.

It was those cheekbones and luminous green eyes of hers.

Isabel made this hairstyle sing.

The first never-fail trick of her trade that Tilly had picked up was this: always pick one feature to accentuate.

One couldn't go accenting the eyes *and* the hair *and* the décolletage *and* the lips *and* everything all the time.

Restraint was the secret.

So, one rationed out the beauty and held some in reserve. In doing so, a mystery was created that would capture the imagination.

In the haut ton every year, a new bevy of bright, young beauties debuted and took their chances in society. And every year—and even at the age of three-and-thirty—Isabel outclassed and outshone them all.

Tilly made sure of it every time Isabel stepped out of the house for those elegant suppers and soirées, those opulent musicales and balls, even a mundane afternoon of social calls and shopping.

"Besides," said Isabel, as Tilly's nimble fingers set to work, "with the general election resolved and the Whigs in charge, Percy wants to understand what this means for the electoral pact with Ireland. Lord Melbourne is rumored to be attending this supper, so I predict much blustering and many deep, whispered conferences." She gave a near-imperceptible shrug of the shoulder. "Percy does like to keep a hand in England's political stew—or a pinky, at least."

Tilly picked up an ivory comb inlaid with mother-of-pearl tulips and considered the best angle for placement.

"Your fellow ain't the sort to give up on a bone once he's got it between his teeth. Old Mr. Bunt had a terrier like that. He'd get a bone and bring it to you all docile like. Then when you'd try to take it, he'd near snap your hand off."

"I'd say my fellow is much like that." Isabel's mouth turned down in a wry smile. "Except I've never seen him bite anyone—*yet*."

To Tilly's mind, the thing about Lord Percival—though Lady Percival was Isabel to her, Lord Percival would always be Lord Percival—was that he'd been a spy for over a decade.

And once a spy, always a spy.

No two ways about it that she could see.

So, he was probably keeping more than a pinky in.

If a person was good at their occupation and they liked it—and clearly Lord Percival was both of those things, but especially the former, as he was still amongst the living despite all that spying—then why would they ever stop?

Isabel reached for the thin stack of correspondence on the dressing table and began picking through. "Oh," she said, her voice brightening, "a letter from Eva."

Eva was Isabel's sister who'd up and married a French marquis—*twice*.

"What's the news from France?" Tilly angled the comb as she slid it into Isabel's hair above the chignon.

"Let's see," said Isabel. "Lucien and the children are well."

Little devilish angels were Eva's sprigs.

Like their mother in no small way, come to think of it.

"They coming for a visit soon?"

Isabel nodded, distracted as she kept reading. "After the new year, once the crossing is calm… The Paris shop is doing so well, they can't keep up with orders."

No surprise there.

A decade ago, Isabel and Eva Galante had arrived in London with little more than a few quid in their pockets and some sewing needles. With no more than that and each other, they'd hung their sign and started sewing dresses. But as their pa had been none other than tailor to the King of Spain, that skill and spirit had been in their blood, hadn't it? And now *Galante: Dressmakers Extraordinaire* had thriving shops in both London and Paris, with Isabel holding up the numbers side of it and Eva the artistic.

An inspiration, those sisters were.

So inspirational, they'd given Tilly an idea of her own, in fact.

Isabel held up a letter with the wax seal intact. "This one's for you."

Sure enough, it was addressed to *Miss Tilly Birdwell*. Tilly recognized the seal, too. The emblem of a needle pulling thread through fabric. This letter was from her bosom friend Nell, who not three years ago became no less a personage than the Duchess of Amherst.

Nell, who had once been a wet nurse.

Nell, who had once been a dressmaker.

Nell, to whom the Galante sisters had also held a hand out and said, "*Come with me.*"

Nell, a duchess.

Tilly tucked the letter into the waistband of her skirt. She would read it over a hot cup of tea later.

Read.

The reading of a letter was a notion that had once stood outside the realm of possibility for an East End gel like Tilly Birdwell. Then a few years ago, Nell had encouraged and taught her her letters.

Tilly had definitely gotten above herself with that leap.

She took a step back and tipped her head this way, then that, making sure the back of Isabel's coiffure was symmetrical and smooth, before she noticed another letter in Isabel's hand. A letter with swirly, gold-embossed print. Tilly whistled. "That's a fancy one, ain't it?"

Even in her elevated life, the occasional *ain't* slipped out.

All right, more than the occasional.

It was just that most of the time when she said *isn't*, it really did feel like she was putting on airs.

Isabel gave a dismissive shrug. "An invitation to a masquerade ball."

"You ain't going?" Tilly asked, but she already knew the answer.

Isabel dropped the invitation into the silver rubbish bin beneath the dressing table. "I never was one for a masquerade."

Tilly lifted a saucy eyebrow. "You and Lord Percival could have a little wild night."

Isabel met Tilly's gaze in the mirror. "And who's to say Lord Percival and I *don't* enjoy a little wild night on occasion?"

With great difficulty, Tilly suppressed the giggle that wanted out.

"In private," said Isabel with a waggle of her own saucy eyebrow.

Now, the giggle was out, and Isabel was laughing along, too, as she came to her feet. "I can practically hear the impatient tap of Percy's foot from here. Am I made up to your satisfaction, *cariña*?"

Tilly stepped back and viewed Isabel from every angle. She picked up a small pot of lanolin she'd subtly tinted and dabbed Isabel's lips and cheekbones. "Now, there you are. The most beautiful lady in Brighton."

Isabel shook her head, smiling. "Oh, Tilly, I'm no rival to *you*."

Tilly took her meaning. She was one of those gels that men liked with her blonde curls, blue eyes, and—well, there was no other way of putting it—*voluptuousness*. She wasn't one of those classical beauties she so admired. Those ladies who were beautiful in paintings and poetry… ladies to be respected and revered from afar.

Tilly's beauty was the sort men liked to put into practice.

She'd left *that* behind nine years ago, too.

She engaged in flirtation, but naught else when it came to the male sex.

Tilly settled an ivory lace shawl on Isabel's shoulders.

With a smile of farewell, Isabel departed, and Tilly set about her nightly duties—folding and putting clothes away; turning down the sheets and fluffing pillows; laying a night chemise on top of the coverlet. Tilly wouldn't see

Isabel again until morning. It was Lord Percival who performed the bedtime duty of unlacing his wife.

And Tilly got an uninterrupted night's sleep.

It was no exaggeration to say these last nine years of her life were better than the sixteen years that had preceded them. The list went on…

She had security.

She even had savings.

She could read.

She could almost talk like a nob.

She'd traveled all over—and not just to Brighton. She'd been to Paris, France…Rome and Venice in Italy…even Geneva with its beautiful lake.

So good life had been these last nine years, she'd even found time to come up with a little dream for herself.

She couldn't sew a dress beyond darning or construct a hat from straw, but she did know what looked agreeable on a woman, from colors to fabrics to draping to hair to hats…*everything*. Isabel had told her she had a gift for it, but Tilly had never truly believed her…until Isabel started reading to her from the gossip rags about Lady Percival Bretagne's impeccable style. Which was the true reason Tilly decided to learn to read—so she could take in that gossip for herself.

And it was true.

Through Isabel, Tilly was setting style for the haut ton.

Lawks.

And the idea had struck her as sure as a lightning bolt.

She could open a shop for women of all sorts to come and pick up some advice on how to look their best—

proper ladies…lady's maids…other women, too. Women who wanted to stand out and shine for their wedding day or a fancy party. Even women who wanted nothing more than to look their best just walking down the street.

Tilly could advise them all.

It didn't have to be a mere dream.

In fact, she'd come up with a plan for opening that shop.

Fifteen years from now.

She would be forty then.

Which wasn't so very long, when one thought about it.

After all, hadn't she been in this life for nine years already?

She even had a dream location for the shop—Burlington Arcade.

Though she knew that one would have to stay up there in the realm of fantasy.

Lords didn't lease those fancy shops to the likes of her.

So, she would be patient and continue creating relationships with shop owners and other lady's maids…learning more about her craft and refining it…making sure every time Isabel stepped out of the house, she was the most beautiful and stylish lady in any room.

Tilly had set about straightening the dressing table when a glint of gold caught the edge of her eye. It was that fancy masquerade invitation in the rubbish bin. Incited the imagination, a masquerade ball did—*mystery…glamour… champagne.*

On a quick—and naughty—impulse, she lifted the invitation from the bin.

> *Lord and Lady Beresford*
> *request the honor of*
> *Lord and Lady Percival's company*
> *at our Saints and Sinners masqued ball*
> *on the evening of*
> *the fifth of November*
> *at the*
> *Royal Pavilion*
> *Guests are to remain unrevealed until midnight*

A glittery shiver tingled up her spine.

The fifth of November...

Tonight.

An idea both sparked and formed in the same instant.

She had time.

She could attend this masquerade ball.

This year for her birthday, Eva had presented her with a black velvet dress trimmed with gold lace from her atelier in Paris. The gift had stolen the breath from Tilly's lungs. That was how exquisite it was.

When she'd thanked Eva, the other woman had smiled in that intense way of hers—no one could match Eva for intensity—and said, "Every woman should have such a dress in her wardrobe. But Tilly?"

"Aye?"

"You must promise to wear it."

Tilly had nodded her agreement.

And she'd kept her promise—though it had only been in the privacy of her room.

Still, she brought it with her when she traveled with Isabel, in case an opportunity ever arose for her to wear it.

Never had that opportunity arisen until…*now*.

Nervy anticipation skittered through her veins and had her all lit up on the inside. If she legged it this minute, she just had time before the shops closed. Her mind began ticking off a list of necessities for such an evening—hooded cloak…silk mask…satin slippers of the sort worn by ladies for their fancy evenings out. These last nine years, she'd only worn sturdy leather boots.

For here was the reason her plan was unimpeachable—a word Lord Percival liked to use—as long as she left the ball before the unmasking at midnight, no one would ever know.

Then a few days later, she would leave Brighton with Lord Percival and Isabel and return to London with no one the wiser.

No one except her, of course.

And the memory of her first—and last—masquerade ball she would forever carry with her and treasure.

She could dance and drink champagne and have herself a little wild night.

How much trouble could she get into, anyway?

2

LATER

Rhys hadn't begun the evening intending to attend a masquerade ball.

He'd started the evening, improbably, at a rather serious-minded supper party.

But that was the thing about the Brighton season—which came after the London season and lasted from late summer through Christmas—one generally accepted invitations to balls and parties one would have ignored in London.

Which was how Rhys had found himself seated at a table at a supper party surrounded by all the preeminent politicians of the day, including none other than the Prime Minister, Lord Melbourne.

Even as Rhys himself had not a lick of interest in politics.

Even as he knew this to be a serious failing of his character.

Well, it was but one of many.

He'd long accepted that fact.

However, Lord Percival Bretagne had been at this particular supper party. A serious-minded man himself, Bretagne wasn't a usual comrade of Rhys's. But Bretagne had a reputation whispered about him—*shadowy dealings in the past...perhaps in the present, too.* And as Bretagne was a friend of a friend of a friend, and Rhys had needed someone well-versed in shadowy dealings, he'd called on Bretagne and laid his problem at the man's feet. He'd been that desperate.

And luck of all luck, Bretagne hadn't dismissed him out of hand. He'd listened and told Rhys he'd see what he could do. He would be in contact.

That was a year ago.

And in the intervening year, Rhys had heard nothing.

Until tonight.

Until from across the dining table, Bretagne had looked him straight in the eye and spoken thirteen fateful words— *Sir Felix will be attending the masquerade ball tonight at the Royal Pavilion.*

The trajectory of Rhys's night switched direction in an instant. He'd stood abruptly, claiming stomach disrupt, and hastily scarpered, leaving fifty sets of lifted eyebrows in his wake. Of course, they might've expected as much, given it was Lord Rhys Osborne causing the kerfuffle.

Rhys had a reputation.

One, admittedly, he'd earned.

The thing was, he'd been invited to that ball. The invitation had surely made its way to every lord and lady presently in Brighton. As the son of an earl, Rhys counted.

Even if he was only a third son.

So, here he was stepping into the Royal Pavilion at ten in the evening. Beyond its grandiosity, this palace was something of an interesting hodgepodge of India-come-to-England. As if it were an Englishman's vision of the subcontinent's grandeur that he would never see firsthand, but had studied in reports and paintings. In fact, Rhys supposed that was exactly what the Royal Pavilion was—King George IV's dream of Indian splendor. A fever dream, really, with its onion domes and minarets that were neither entirely Indian nor English, but a style all their own.

As Rhys approached the front entrance, he adjusted his thin black mask and presented the footmen guarding the door with the invitation he'd stopped by his hotel to retrieve. Granted entry with a nod and a murmured, "My lord," Rhys stepped into the dimly lit interior, music from stringed instruments wafting through the air, every dark corner an invitation for close conversation.

Of course, that was entirely the point of a masquerade ball—*close conversation...intrigue...amorous pursuits...decadence*. Riding along the edge of the music came laughter, too, and gaiety. A feeling of spontaneity sparked through the air, as if anything could happen at any moment—*possibility*.

A feeling that lifted one out of one's life for a night.

One didn't have to be oneself.

One could be anyone.

Of course, dawn would inevitably arrive—and, with it, bleary-eyed reality.

But at ten in the evening, the night was crisp and young.

Dawn—and reality—were hours away.

Except, this wasn't the narrative Rhys's night would follow.

He wasn't here for decadence or gaiety or amorous pursuits.

He'd had enough of those to last him a lifetime.

He was here for Sir Felix Mortimer.

But, really, he was here for redemption.

That was the possibility that lay at the heart of this night for him.

As he wound through opulent, gilded rooms done in the chinoiserie decor so popular in the last century, Rhys caught the light of recognition in several pairs of masked eyes and experienced not an iota of surprise. He was tall and broad-shouldered, black-haired and silver-eyed. He'd stood out in a crowd all his life.

But that wasn't the only reason he would've been recognized.

He would've been expected, as in the eyes of Society, he was a waster and a rake.

And wasters and rakes liked masquerade balls, didn't they?

He lifted a coupe of champagne off a passing tray—and didn't touch his lips to it.

That was the important thing.

He didn't have a problem with drink, as such.

But he did have a problem with the paths drink led him down.

So, he'd learned at the beginning of this long last year to accept one drink and nurse it all night, unimbibed.

The thing about becoming a waster and a rake—and he'd had many sober hours…days…weeks…months to contemplate this—it was born in the lap of success. All it took was one good run at the cards and the dice and the women.

That was how the slide into dissolution began.

It began with winning.

And he'd won—for years.

Then at some point he hadn't noticed, he'd stopped winning.

And that had gone on for years, too.

Until a year ago.

It had been the end of the quarter and his stipend for the next three months hadn't yet arrived in his bank account, but he'd wanted a usual night out. So, he'd walked into Papa's study and taken his signet ring, which he would use to gain entry into a game, then earn it back. Come morning, he would've replaced it back in Papa's desk drawer, with no one ever the wiser.

That night hadn't even been the first time he'd done it.

Except that night, he hadn't earned it back.

He'd lost it to Sir Felix Mortimer in a game of Loo.

But that hadn't been the true low point of his career as a waster and a rake.

It had been the confession to Papa, for he'd had to confess, otherwise loyal servants would've come under suspicion for theft.

Papa hadn't shouted. He'd listened quietly. Then once

Rhys finished, he'd expressed disappointment and resignation and not one ounce of surprise that his third son had done such a thing as gamble away his signet ring on a hand of cards.

It was Papa's lack of surprise and utter resignation that had been Rhys's nadir—and what had turned his life around one hundred and eighty degrees.

However, turning one's life around and finding purpose was a more challenging pursuit than it looked from the outside. He wasn't soldier material, and he certainly wasn't fit for the church. *Business…* He liked the sound of it, but he didn't have any ideas or skills, as such.

The fact was he'd excelled at being a waster and a rake. With his looks and charm, he had all the natural gifts for the pursuit, really. Simply, something got in his blood when he was holding cards…spinning a wheel…tossing dice…bedding a woman…

He shook the thought away.

He would reach his thirtieth birthday next year.

He truly needed to get something going.

But Sir Felix had to be dealt with first.

After the rotter won the ring off Rhys, he'd taken himself straight across the channel and to the Continent, where he'd begun blatantly flaunting the Earl of Ashburn's signet ring and bragging to every available ear that he'd won it off the earl's waster son, Lord Rhys Osborne.

Which he'd been doing for the last year.

So, Rhys had sought out the whispered skills of a friend of a friend of a friend—*Lord Percival Bretagne*—who had counseled patience and clean living. He'd also confirmed for Rhys something he'd suspected—that Sir Felix was a card cheat, which, even as it made Rhys's blood boil, had come as no surprise.

With no alternative available to him, Rhys had exercised patience and clean living with a few unbreakable rules for himself…

No drinking.

No gambling.

No more married women…or women, in general.

His appetites were too strong, for he'd realized women —*the flirting…the chase…the consummation*—were an addiction, too.

It had been a long, hard year.

He entered the banqueting room, which had been transformed for the night into a ballroom with dozens of couples swirling across the gleaming dancing floor beneath the warm sparkle of blazing chandeliers. He moved along the periphery like a shadow, his eye scanning the tops of heads for Sir Felix's bald patch or the flash of emerald from Papa's signet ring.

Ahead, a vibrant blonde surrounded by a crush of men snagged his eye. She was wearing a mask, of course, but not much else that would leave anything to the imagination. A dramatic black-and-gold creation, the bottom half of the dress was wide and floaty in the typical style of a ballgown, but the top half was a different matter altogether, fitted to her as if it were a second skin. Actually, the dress provided ample coverage, but the body beneath it simply wouldn't be contained—*curvy…lush…* She was the sort of woman men vied with each other over—which was, in fact, what the gentlemen surrounding her were presently doing.

And the woman?

Her laughter betrayed not an ounce of care.

A year ago, Rhys would've tossed his hat into that ring —and he would've prevailed.

The reasons were simple and immutable.

He was a lord.

He was handsome.

He was charming.

And he was a rake known to be endowed with certain gifts.

What could he say?

Word got around about that sort of thing.

Two or three or ten drinks, and she would've been a path he'd gone down—literally.

His cock filled to half-mast at the very thought.

He gave himself a mental shake.

He could hardly blame his cock though, could he?

It *had* been a year.

He dragged his gaze away from the woman and the chase unpursued.

Sir Felix wouldn't be in this room, anyway.

As the blonde was led onto the dancing floor, her curls bouncing with delight—other parts of her, too—Rhys wove his way through the crowd and into the Grand Salon that for this night was the gaming room. Every card game one could think of was being played beneath its sky-blue domed ceiling—Piquet...Whist...Faro...Commerce... Vingt-et-Un...*Loo*.

At a corner table, Rhys spied a familiar shiny patch of bald head.

Sir Felix Mortimer.

Anticipation flared through him.

There, at that table, sat his opportunity to make things right for the first time in his adult life.

In an attempt to make his presence as unobtrusive as possible—a challenge given his height of six feet and two inches in his bare feet—Rhys moved along the wall until he stood only a few yards from Sir Felix's table. He saw with no small amount of mean satisfaction that this last year hadn't treated Sir Felix well. Sure, he was still in possession of that specific public-school handsomeness that had been bred into him by noble forebears. But Sir Felix had picked up some premature lines on his forehead...a subtle note of strain about his mouth and the corners of his eyes.

One thing was the same, however.

Sir Felix remained the smug, smarmy cheat Rhys remembered from a year ago.

And there came another pulse of that fury that had his hands curling into fists.

He experienced a moment's pause. What was his plan, anyway? To watch and catch Sir Felix out for a card cheat for all to hear and witness?

For here was the thing: as far as Rhys had been able to see over the last few tricks, Sir Felix had betrayed not a single tell.

Which allowed for a possibility Rhys didn't much like.

Could it have been that Sir Felix had beaten him fair

and square when he'd taken Papa's signet ring off him a year ago?

The hand now over, and having passed the deck of cards to the player on his left to deal, Sir Felix's gaze lifted and met Rhys's. Those slitted blue depths held not the faintest whisper of surprise. This last year, he'd been expecting Rhys.

He lifted his hand and scratched his cheek with his pinky, the cabochon emerald flashing brilliant green in the chandelier light.

The rotter smirked—and Rhys knew.

A year ago, Sir Felix Mortimer had cheated.

And tonight Rhys would prove it—and get his father's signet ring back.

"If it isn't Lord Rhys Osborne behind that mask, I'll eat my hat," said Sir Felix to a few chuckles around the table. "It's been—*what?*—a year since we last met?"

Rhys's teeth wanted to grind together. He didn't let them, as all eyes appeared riveted by the long-coming confrontation.

"I seem to remember you enjoy a bit of Loo," continued the rotter to yet more chuckling. "Care to join us for a few hands?"

Rhys couldn't say *no*.

And there were a few reasons why.

First, there was his reputation as a known wastrel and rake.

A wastrel and rake wouldn't say *no* to a few hands of cards.

And second, if he said *no*, he would have to take himself elsewhere.

He wasn't doing that.

Not without the ring.

So, he curved his mouth into the semblance of a rakish angle—an angle that felt creaky and decidedly out of practice—and took the empty seat to the right of Sir Felix. But as he lowered into the chair, something unexpected happened.

A few seats to the other side of Sir Felix, the vibrant blonde he'd noticed in the ballroom joined the table, her markers already out. She was the sort of woman one's eyes had difficulty deciding where to look. A veritable buffet of a woman, the brighter light of the card room confirmed.

Rhys exhaled a rough breath and fixed his gaze directly in front of him.

He couldn't allow himself to become distracted.

Sir Felix held no such reservations as he allowed his gaze to indulge in a thorough sweep of the blonde.

Rhys cleared his throat.

Sir Felix's gaze shifted to meet Rhys's without the faintest hint of abashment. He slid the deck of cards over. "Why don't you deal first?"

Rhys grunted and accepted the deck. He didn't want the first deal. He wanted Sir Felix to deal, so he could get on with exposing the man for the cheat he was and take the ring back.

While Rhys shuffled the cards, Sir Felix asked, "Three or five card Loo?"

"Three."

Each of the six players seated at the table tossed three markers into the center pool.

"And shall we play unlimited?" A dare glittered in Sir Felix's eyes.

Instinct had Rhys wanting to say *no*, but he couldn't. Simply because the Rhys he'd been his entire adult life until a year ago would've said… "What's the point of playing any other way?"

Limited Loo kept the pool fixed and the stakes low. With unlimited Loo, however, the pool only increased and increased as looed players—those players who stayed in play and lost all three tricks in a hand—were required to match the pool as their pay-in for the next hand, causing the value of the pool to balloon into dangerously high stakes within a few hands. Lords had lost everything from prized racehorses to unentailed country estates to their father's emerald signet ring in the course of an hour of unlimited Loo.

Rhys dealt three cards to each player. As Sir Felix was seated to Rhys's left, he led the first trick with an ace of diamonds, making diamonds the suit as the other players followed. The blonde, Rhys noticed, played a queen of spades, which meant she had no diamonds in her hand. As Rhys was the dealer, he was last to play his card—ten of diamonds.

Now, it was time to reveal the trump card.

As all the players except the blonde had followed suit, if the card was a diamond, club, or heart, Sir Felix would take the trick.

Rhys flipped the card.

Seven of spades.

Because she'd played the queen, the blonde took the trick.

A smile twitched about her lush lips that appeared tinted with a touch of rouge, and above her black silk mask, her eyebrows waggled with barely suppressed mischief.

At least someone was having a good time.

As the second trick played out, Rhys experienced déjà vu as he lost—*again.* Except it wasn't the blonde who won this time, but some other chap. However, one dim flicker of light in the darkness was that Sir Felix hadn't yet taken a trick, either—which meant he might start cheating.

On the third trick, however, Sir Felix remedied his losing situation and won—without cheating, as far as Rhys could tell.

Rhys and two others had looed the hand, which meant they each had to pay in the sum of the pool from the last hand, which the three winners were now splitting amongst themselves.

And like that, the stakes took on an altogether different timbre.

No longer was the game light and fun.

The game was now serious business.

Rhys saw that fact acknowledged within every pair of eyes at the table.

Well, everyone except the blonde, who didn't appear to take anything seriously.

As Sir Felix was the player to Rhys's left, it was now his deal. Rhys passed him the deck. If the rotter were going to cheat, this hand would be his best opportunity as dealer.

While Rhys watched Sir Felix shuffle the cards and cut sideways smirks his way and leers the blonde's, a vision of the man Rhys had been a year ago came to him. A man in his late twenties who was still living like the lordling he'd been in his early twenties. What had been sowing his wild oats in those earlier years had transitioned into something less fun and less socially palatable. At some point, without Rhys noticing, wild had tipped into wastrel.

That was the man who had sat across the table from Sir Felix a year ago.

A reckless waster…an easy target.

And that was the man Sir Felix thought he was sitting beside tonight.

Sir Felix dealt them each three cards.

This hand had both some key similarities to the previous hand and some key differences.

A chap across the table took one trick.

The blonde took two tricks.

Rhys looed—*again*—as did a few others.

And one of those others who'd looed happened to have been Sir Felix.

The thought occurred to Rhys that Sir Felix and the blonde were in league to run the table. But, *no*, the scowl trenched across Sir Felix's high forehead told a different story as, with eyes narrowed, he watched the blonde divide the pool with the other chap, two to one.

Rhys found himself at a crossroads.

The pool, as he'd predicted from the start, had

ballooned. The buy-in was now over £100, which wasn't prohibitively expensive, but enough to give one pause.

But he'd come this far, and what was the alternative?

Leave the table? Abandon the ring?

No.

However, he'd come prepared. From an interior coat pocket, he pulled a scrap of paper and a pencil. He scrawled *£100* across the surface and tossed the vowel into the pool. "This should suffice, no?"

Levelly, he met Sir Felix's gaze, then lifted an eyebrow for good measure.

Rhys knew it was now his own eye glinting with a dare.

A trio of seconds ticked past with Sir Felix on the spot. Then Rhys watched as if from a dream as the rotter tugged Papa's signet ring off his pinky and dropped it into the pool. "And I reckon *that* will suffice."

The blonde, shuffling the deck, as it was her deal, said, "Yeah, I reckon it will."

The blonde...

In all Rhys's predicted scenarios for how this night could twist and turn, he hadn't accounted for *her*.

Plainly, she was having a night.

Which was slightly infuriating in and of itself, for she didn't seem to care all that much.

It was as if she would've been just as happy losing.

Like it was all a lark to her.

Rhys felt his back teeth grind together.

She dealt the cards.

He looked at his cards. Objectively speaking, he held a hand that wasn't precisely terrible, but legitimately bad.

Judging by the undiminished scowl on Sir Felix's face, his hand wasn't any better.

And the blonde kept smiling in that carefree way of hers.

So, who knew.

One couldn't read her.

The player to her left led the first trick with a queen of diamonds. Rhys played the ten, and Sir Felix the king.

And the blonde… Of course, she played the ace.

She flipped the trump card—*three of diamonds.*

The blonde took the first trick.

Sir Felix had gone a subtle shade of green, his skin looking as though a sheen of sweat had slicked a thin layer across his body.

Rhys knew the signs, for the same thing was happening to him.

What in the blazes was going on?

For the second trick, a seven of spades was played. Rhys had no choice but to follow with the eight. Sir Felix played the jack. The blonde didn't follow suit and instead played the jack of diamonds.

The breath seemed to have been sucked out of this corner of the room.

Word of a high-stakes game tended to get around.

The trump card flipped…

Two of diamonds.

The blonde won—*again.*

Though Rhys felt this night slipping away, he understood he still had a chance to win Papa's ring.

Everything—his entire life, it felt in this moment—hung on the next trick.

If he managed to take it, he would use all the skills and charm in his armory to convince the blonde to take everything in the pool, including his £100 vowel, but leave him the ring.

Besides, he'd saved his best card for last.

Further, he felt the wind of good fortune blowing his way when the trick opened with the jack of hearts.

The blood roaring through his veins, sweat coating his palms, on the brink of redemption—*at last*—he played the king of hearts.

Face utterly impassive, Sir Felix flipped the ace of clubs. As he couldn't play the suit, he would be praying for the trump card to be clubs.

At last, it was the blonde's turn.

She flipped her card.

Staring up from green baize for all to see was none other than the ace of hearts.

Time stopped, and suddenly it was as if Rhys had wool in his ears.

He blinked, the plain facts of the situation refusing to register.

He hadn't won—and neither had Sir Felix.

Meanwhile, the blonde was going around the table and exchanging markers for guineas. She was cashing out.

Then it was her laughter filling the air and floating in her wake as she exited the room, her step light and devastatingly joyful.

Flabbergasted, Rhys met Sir Felix's smirk. "Thought

tonight was your night, eh?" And the rotter laughed, making it clear he'd never cared about the ring. But he'd sure had fun needling Rhys with it, hadn't he?

Rhys shot to his feet. With the blonde gone, he was at risk of losing the ring forever.

No, no, no.

He could not let that happen.

He would not let that happen.

His feet were on the move. He wasn't sure how, but *somehow* the blonde had cheated. No one had that kind of luck.

Oh, *yes*, he would find her, and she would tell him what her game was.

And she would give him the ring.

Tonight—*this entire last year*—would not be a complete loss.

He understood it wouldn't fully redeem him in Papa's eyes, but it was a start.

What level of hell had that bubbly blonde card sharp come from, anyway?

3

———

Tilly stepped into the awe-inducing ballroom of the Royal Pavilion and thought she'd gotten more than she'd bargained for when she'd embarked upon this little wild night.

She'd gotten the best night of her life.

This masquerade ball was everything she'd ever dreamed a masquerade ball would be—sumptuous, opulent, and mysterious, with all these aristocrats decked out in their finest. It was clear they all recognized each other behind their masks and were playing a big game of pretend of not knowing each other.

But wasn't that the point?

How could a little wild night be had if one was being their ordinary, old self?

With a mask on, anyone could be anyone.

Even her.

It was freedom—and it was fun.

And, *lawks*, the champagne. How it flowed without end.

And the dancing, *oh*, the dancing…

She loved to dance, and she'd had no shortage of men—*lords*—vying for her hand.

Her, a lady's maid.

But they didn't know that, did they? As long as she kept her mouth mostly shut—one dropped *aitch* and the jig would've been up—she could be anyone. These lords didn't know Tilly Birdwell from Eve of Garden-of-Eden fame, and she didn't know any of them, either.

Well, that wasn't strictly true.

An hour ago, there'd been one lord she'd recognized.

She would've known him anywhere, even after nine years, for he'd made promises to her once.

None of which he'd kept, if she was keeping score.

Sir Felix Mortimer.

She'd even come face to face with him.

And though she'd felt her heart in her throat, his gaze hadn't lingered on her for even the split of a second—not like it once had.

Not like when she was sixteen.

At five and twenty, she reckoned she was now too advanced in years for his tastes.

And though she'd been whirling across the ballroom floor in a waltz, she'd managed to keep an eye on him until he disappeared into a room that she'd known was the card room.

She'd given it a few more dances. A bit of time to talk herself out of what she knew she would do, anyway.

But it wasn't long before the little devil perched on her shoulder won, and she'd wandered into the card room, where she found Sir Felix playing Loo—a card game he'd taught her.

He'd taught her all his tricks, too.

She'd sat at the table, bold as she pleased, and all but dared him to recognize her.

He hadn't.

And there was that irresistible urge, spurring her on, tempting her to beat him at his own game. After all, she had a few guineas. Hard-earned guineas, lest she forget the realities. But they were guineas she could lose and only be set back by a few months toward her dream. What was fifteen years plus six months, anyway?

So, she'd cobbled a hasty plan together. If she lost at the start, she would chalk it up to an experience and walk away.

But she hadn't lost.

She'd won—and kept winning.

Until she'd won one hundred and thirty-four guineas— *one hundred and thirty-four guineas!*—and a £100 vowel off some flush lord and a large gold ring with a big oval-cut, cabochon emerald in the center. The vowel was nothing to her. She wouldn't be able to redeem it, as she wasn't about to waste time haggling with an aristocrat. But that ring… It was a lord's ring.

Would fetch a pretty penny, that ring.

By her rough estimation, this night had brought her years closer to opening her shop.

Years.

Her feet hadn't touched earth these last ten minutes.

She came to a stop at the edge of the dancing floor. She wanted to dance—and she wouldn't have to wait long to be asked.

There was just something about her.

She knew—and had accepted—this about herself. Men could never resist trying it on with her, as if their noses were specially attuned to her scent. In her former line of work, it had made her quite a few guineas. Guineas she'd had no choice but to earn.

Not if she'd wanted a roof over her head and food in her belly.

Not if she'd wanted to stay out of the workhouse.

Maybe if, when she'd been given the choice between Pizzy's Pleasure Palace and St. Mary Magdalen Workhouse, she'd known what-all earning a guinea at Pizzy's, then Number 9, would've been all about, she would've chosen the workhouse. But she'd been all of fourteen years old, and it had been in Pizzy's interests to let her discover those details for herself.

And by then, it was too late, wasn't it?

She was a strumpet.

She closed her eyes, inhaled deeply, then exhaled it all out, like she'd taught herself to do when those thoughts and memories came at her. And these last nine years that she'd been out of that life, it helped when she wanted to be in the here and now.

Her eyes opened—to find a crescent of men assembled

before her, waiting for her to choose which would lead her onto the dancing floor.

The *who* didn't matter much.

She simply wanted to dance until her feet could fall off.

Or, more like, until the clock struck eleven fifty-nine and she would scud it out of here before the grand unmasking.

She reckoned she had a quarter of an hour until then.

She reached out to accept a hand. Only, just before it clasped around hers, a large male form stepped into that sliver of empty space and took her hand, instead. Her head had to tip back to get a good look at the fellow. He was tall and broad-shouldered…dark hair that shone black…and though he was wearing a mask, with his strong jaw, straight nose, and lips on the lush side, she could tell he was handsome and used to command…a *lord*.

Definitely a lord.

Behind his black mask, his eyes held a silvery light, as his other hand settled on her ribs and he pulled her closer. And those eyes staring down at her as he whirled them into the *one-two-three* of the waltz… Well, they were observing her with more intensity than this moment strictly warranted.

Instinctively, she made to retract her hand and pull away from him altogether—she was no lady, so she wasn't under some obligation to dance with any old rotter who chose to dance with her—but he held firm as he kept them in time to the music.

A stunning, undeniable fact assailed her. His lack of manners aside, this lord could dance. Not a hint of stiffness in him as he led them around the ballroom. Fluid and utterly at ease in his body, he was a dance partner of the divine variety. A woman could be convinced she was dancing on air in his arms.

Except…there was something in the way he wasn't taking his eyes off her.

It unsettled.

It unnerved.

It prevented her from giving over to the pleasure of this dance.

"Do I know you?"

She had to ask, for a possibility tickled at the back of her mind.

A possibility she didn't much like.

This lord might've known her from her previous life.

But wasn't that unlikely? It had been nine years, and she was a full-fledged woman now, wasn't she?

"That's a sharp game of Loo you play," he said, his voice a deep, velvet rumble. The sort of voice that might send a shiver racing up a woman's spine if she wasn't careful.

Or even if she was.

Then the content of his words hit her, followed in the next second by recognition.

Oh.

This lord had been one of the other players in the game of Loo.

In truth, she hadn't been paying attention to him, so focused she'd been on Sir Felix. She'd sized this man up for just another handsome lord and hadn't thought anything about him since. She made it an express point not to think about handsome lords. They were the ones who could completely upend a chit's goals and aspirations. She'd seen it happen, time and oft—had even been on the verge of it happening to her that once with Sir Felix—and it wasn't about to happen to her at this stage in her life.

She could only think of one response. "Thank you."

His gaze narrowed. "It wasn't a compliment."

A laugh startled out of her. "Why is that?"

"You're a cheat."

She supposed the *tricks* Sir Felix had taught her all them years ago could've been construed as *cheating*. She began calculating. "You're the fellow with the hundred-pound vowel."

"Aye."

Her mind made up in an instant, she lifted her hand off his shoulder and dipped quick fingers into the valley between her breasts, which emerged clutching the slip of paper. "*Here*. Yours free and clear."

Given the lift of the fellow's brow, she reckoned she'd shocked him. Well, lords were easily shocked, weren't they?

Reluctantly, he accepted the note and shoved it into a coat pocket.

She wasn't finished. "And how much more did I take off you?"

She wanted no remaining ties between her and this too-handsome and too-intense lord after the final note of this dance echoed through the air. Until he'd taken her hand, she'd been having the best night of her life. And though she hated to give up even a penny of the one hundred and thirty-four pounds weighing heavy in her reticule, she didn't see how she had much of a choice.

She didn't need a lord hounding her heels.

"Pardon?" he asked.

"How much more did I take off you? Fifty pounds and call it even?"

"*Fifty pounds?*"

"I know for a fact that I took more off the others, but I'll be generous—fifty-five."

That would leave her with seventy-nine pounds—and the ring.

His jaw tensed and released. "Did you know Sir Felix before tonight?"

She laughed—and she didn't much like that laugh. It sounded wholly composed of bitterness. The sort of laugh that corroded from the inside. In her previous line of employment, she'd been acquainted with that laugh from the older strumpets.

Of a sudden, a loud, blustery voice that Tilly once knew all too well cut through the music and gaiety, "I knew I knew you from somewhere. By gads, I knew it!"

She felt a hand on her shoulder, pulling her and her irritatingly intense dance partner to a full stop. The next second, she was face to face with Sir Felix. Though he was wearing a mask, there was no mistaking the mean glint in his eye that he used to get. And to think once she'd believed him the handsomest man in the world…

"Now," he bellowed, his voice ripe with drunken belligerence, "what was your name again?"

Like that, the magic of the night vanished once and for all.

There would be no getting it back.

Tilly felt like an animal whose foot had been snared in a trap.

Run, urged the little animal being inside her. *Run as fast as your legs can go…run!*

And that was exactly what she did.

She shook off the hands of both of these men who each wanted something from her—nothing she felt inclined to part with voluntarily—and she let that little animal being take over and she ran, paying no heed to the bodies she muscled through and shouldered past…the rooms and corridors she dashed through that only a few hours ago had gobsmacked her with awe…the newly purchased cloak she was leaving behind… *Nothing* was going to stand between her and freedom.

Outside and through the garden lit by sporadically hung lanterns and the twinkling stars above, she made a series of lefts and rights through the Royal Pavilion's grounds until she reached the street, then it was more lefts and rights down streets she didn't know until she was certain she didn't hear the heavy, rhythmic thud of male footsteps behind her. At last, she slowed her pace, her lungs struggling to catch her breath, her mind racing to gather her bearings.

And while she might not have the least idea where her feet had led her, a small cheer of triumph wouldn't quiet down and she realized she was smiling.

Couldn't stop, in fact.

The little animal being inside her had never failed her in the past, and it hadn't tonight, either.

An amazed laugh erupted from her.

Sir Felix.

Well, wasn't he a ghost from the past come to life?

And, *oh*, didn't it feel just that good to have gotten something off him. A corrective balancing of the scales, as she saw it.

But her mind had no interest in tarrying on Sir Felix.

It was that other gent it wanted to linger over.

Now that she had a moment to properly reflect, what had been his angle?

With a little breathing room, she considered the possibility that she'd gotten it wrong back in the ballroom. That man hadn't wanted the £100 vowel or the fifty-five pounds.

He'd wanted something else from her.

Well, there was only one other thing men had ever wanted from her—and he wasn't about to get *that*.

A sensation rippled through her, as if her body was holding onto sense memories of him—of his skill at dancing...of the feel of him, all masculine muscle and strength...and the feel of herself in his arms—*warm... tingly...lit up from the inside...* And a stray thought wandered into her mind, and she wondered if, perhaps, he *was* the sort who could get something else from her.

Something that involved more privacy than was afforded on a dancing floor.

She shook her head free of that stray thought, and her

smile returned. There had been a hairy moment, for certain, but it had turned out all right, hadn't it?

Better than all right.

She was the possessor of one hundred and thirty-four pounds and a ring she could sell in London.

She'd wanted a little wild night in Brighton, and hadn't she gotten one?

As her feet pointed in the direction of the hotel, the giggle that floated in her wake could've been heard all the way down to the sea.

4

LONDON, A MONTH LATER

"In my experience of matters such as yours, Osborne," said Lord Percival Bretagne, rising to his feet, "dead ends never stay dead for long."

Rhys reluctantly unfurled his long body and followed his host by coming to a stand, understanding two things at once.

Bretagne had just told him to be patient—and their meeting had reached its conclusion.

Frustration cascaded through Rhys. It had been a month—a *month*—since the night of the masquerade. A month since he'd come *this* close to winning Papa's signet ring back—and lost it...*again*.

And here he was being told to be patient.

He *had* been patient. This last month he'd waited *patiently* for this quarter-hour meeting—only to be told to be more patient.

A quarter of an hour ago, he'd walked into Bretagne's residence, confident the man would have usable information for him. But, no, nothing. He'd essentially told Rhys in indifferently polite terms that when he learned anything new he would contact him, which was a thinly veiled way of telling Rhys to stop sending notes every week asking if he'd happened across any intelligence.

Fair play.

Rhys could accept he'd made a minor nuisance of himself.

It was a different sort of acceptance, however, he'd been dodging.

Papa's signet ring was hopelessly lost.

He needed to accept that.

Except, he couldn't quite.

It could yet turn up at a pawnbroker.

Surely, it would, eventually, for what would the blonde want with it, anyway?

She couldn't wear it.

It was too big.

She'd want the money for it.

Christmas was only a few weeks away. Wouldn't she want the money for a gift?

So, here was hope creeping in again and the inability to accept the loss.

Bretagne strode toward the door, and Rhys had no choice but to follow. Still, he yet had a question to ask. "So, you've known for years that Sir Felix is a card cheat?" He tried to ask offhand, but wasn't sure he succeeded.

Bretagne didn't bother glancing over. "I did." He sounded utterly bored.

"Then why didn't you ever expose him?"

Bretagne met his gaze, his expression both incredulous and slightly amused. "Why would I?"

Righteousness surged through Rhys. A surprising feeling, that, and one he couldn't rightly say he'd experienced in recent years. "Cheating is wrong."

Bretagne smiled—like a wolf. "But it's one waster cheating another waster. I've no dog in that fight."

Rhys felt the sting of Bretagne's words.

A year ago, he was one of those wasters.

Bretagne was, of course, correct in his view.

When they reached the corridor, his host said, "I'm headed the other direction. You know the way out?"

"Aye," said Rhys, taking Bretagne's hand in a parting shake.

Then he was winding down corridors and staircases toward the ground floor and the door that led out a side entrance. Bretagne and his wife occupied a residence in the east wing of the opulent, sprawling mansion belonging to his father, the Duke of Arundel, a practice that was common in aristocratic families. Rhys was, in fact, an outlier in this regard, as several years ago, he'd taken up a flat of rooms on Bennet Street. It wasn't by happenstance that Bennet Street was near his favorite clubs and gaming hells on St. James's Street. A real blessing to the wastrel rake.

Of course, much had changed in the last year.

He was now a reformed wastrel rake.

Or making the attempt, anyway.

It had to count for something, but he was having a difficult time seeing how, for the universe hadn't exactly shown itself in a benevolent mood for his past transgressions. Otherwise, it would tip up Papa's signet ring and indicate all was forgiven, wouldn't it?

But, *nay*, apparently the universe had yet more to teach him, and he had only himself to blame.

How had he let it come to this?

The ring was nowhere.

Even Bretagne, a former and possibly present spymaster, had heard nothing.

Perhaps the blonde and Sir Felix had been in league, after all.

But Rhys had doubts about this theory.

When Sir Felix had approached them on the dancing floor, the panic that had sparked in the blonde's eyes had been genuine. Then she'd been running, and Rhys following. But where she was able to find angles and slip through the crowd, he'd met obstacle after stubborn obstacle—and he'd lost her.

It hadn't been her first time running from a man.

Rhys knew that much.

He knew something else, too.

She wasn't an aristocrat.

Her voice had revealed East-End beginnings.

Then, when he'd returned to the ballroom to confront Sir Felix about how he knew the woman, the rotter had been gone, too.

And Rhys was left with precisely what he'd entered the Royal Pavilion holding—*nothing*.

Outside on the sidewalk, he flipped the collar of his greatcoat against a soggy northern wind that was blowing through, his feet pointed in the direction of Bennet Street. He'd made it ten or so yards when he heard a shout at his back, "*Oi!*"

His feet stuttered to an abrupt stop—and not because he thought the *oi!* intended for him.

He knew that *oi!*

Even from a single syllable.

He whipped around, frantically scanning the pedestrians bustling all around...the carriages and hackney cabs and drays racketing down the street...for a woman with blonde curls and, well, curves.

The next instant, he located...*her.*

Arm still lifted, she was dashing into the street toward the hackney cab that had stopped for her.

Rhys's lungs lost their ability to draw breath. Truly, he couldn't believe what his eyes were telling him. It was *her*—the blonde card cheat he'd been searching for this last month.

Though he was viewing her in daylight for the first time, it could be no other—sun-kissed curls springing free from the chignon at her neck...those curves which not even a woolen winter pelisse could obscure...her smile that sparkled all the way to her eyes... His first impression proved to have been the correct impression: she was no lady. Ladies didn't smile up at hackney cab drivers like that.

Not for the first time, he wondered: how had she secured an invitation to that masquerade ball, anyway?

The mysteries surrounding this woman were certainly mounting.

When she placed a foot on the first step of the carriage, Rhys snapped to.

Oh, no, no, no.

He wasn't losing her again.

No time to spare, his feet were on the move, covering the ground between him and the cab in fewer than ten long strides, and, without a second thought, he was shoving into the conveyance just as her hand was reaching for the handle to close the door.

"Oi!" she exclaimed from her seat on the bench, "what do you think you're—" Her eyes, the clear blue of a rare type of topaz, went wide as saucers. "*You!*"

Only after Rhys had shoved inside the carriage did he realize it was a two-seater. He saw but a single option—to squeeze onto the bench beside her. Even as he attempted to make himself small and shove back into the cramped corner, the fact remained that the entire right side of his body was in full contact with the left side of hers.

Outrage shimmered about her, umbrage twinning with bewilderment in her topaz-blue eyes.

The universe continued to have its fun with him, didn't it?

The cab lurched into motion, and no choice left to him, Rhys got directly to it. "You have something I want."

Her brow crinkled, then a second later, released. "All this over fifty—fifty-*five* pounds? I thought gambling debts were naught but minor annoyances to you lords."

Up until a year ago, Rhys had been precisely that sort of lord, and he couldn't help feeling annoyed that she'd so efficiently hit the bull's-eye of his past character. "Actually," he said, "you took *eighty-four* pounds off me. But that's not why we're here."

She gave her head a slow, incredulous shake. "Is that so?" She didn't wait for his answer. "I know why *I'm* here. You're the one with some explaining to do. There is no *we*."

"The ring."

Her eyes narrowed into irritated blue slits. "Now, I won that ring off Sir Felix, fair and square."

Rhys lifted his brow. "*Fair?*"

"To my way of thinking," she began, looking disinclined to give any ground, "when one cheats a cheat, it ain't cheating."

Rhys exhaled sharply through his nose. She had a point, and it was a good one. Still… "A year ago, Sir Felix cheated it off me."

Understanding lit within her eyes. "And now you want it back."

"Yes."

"And you think I should just give it to you."

"I could pay you for it."

Her head tipped to the side. Nothing in her demeanor said he'd gained an inch of ground, as she didn't appear at all motivated by his offer of money. "What's so special about this ring?"

She held the whip hand—and she knew it.

He was going to have to tell her the significance of the ring. "The ring belonged—*belongs*—to my father."

She scrunched back into her corner and considered him for a long, uncomfortable moment. "And you gambled it away?" It was a question—but only technically.

Just one answer to that question would suffice… "Yes."

Her head tipped to the other side. "You're a nob. Can't you buy him another ring?"

"It's his signet ring."

"*Signet ring?*"

"The sort of ring passed down from father to son."

"So, your pa gave it to you, then?"

"It would've gone to my eldest brother."

Rhys was leaving a great deal unsaid between the lines here, but this woman looked as if she heard every last unspoken word loud and clear—he'd taken the ring without permission, then lost it in a card game.

Like any wastrel lord would.

He saw no option but to divulge yet more information. "My father is an earl."

A faint, possibly cynical smile curved the blonde's mouth, then she whistled. "So, you're a right, proper nob, then."

"*Proper* might be shooting wide of the mark."

A knowing glint shone in her eyes that Rhys didn't like. That glint said she'd seen his type—*the wastrel lord*—and didn't think much of him.

He cleared his throat and aimed for authoritative with his next words. "So, it would be best if you and I came to terms, and you returned the ring."

The reality of the words emerged altogether differently from his intent. He'd been aiming for authoritative, but what hit the air sounded distinctly…*entitled.*

And within that note of entitlement lay an implication

of class imbalance and of the power of an earldom and, for that matter, the entire English aristocracy at his back.

Again, her mouth curved into a little smile, this one, however, holding no trace of humor. She didn't flinch when she said, "Would it now?"

Immediately, Rhys saw his mistake.

And he saw it was too late to right it.

5

Tilly had awakened this morning at her usual time thinking today would be an ordinary day like any other.

Only much better, as it was December and the Christmas season was now fully upon them. She adored Christmas—the anticipation…the merriment…the food… the gifts. Now, she enjoyed receiving a gift as much as the next person, but what she loved most was observing her folk through the year and finding the perfect gifts for them.

So, today was to have been split between lady's-maid errands on Old Bond Street and picking up gifts in Burlington Arcade that she'd ordered special.

The point was she'd had a fun day ahead of her.

Until this man—*a lord*—had muscled and squirmed his way into this cab with her.

Now her fun would have to wait until she'd done something about him.

For here was Brighton, returned like a bad eel pie, in the form of one determined, massive, entitled lord.

She saw what he was trying to do—use his lordly power to bully her. So many lords were bullies, like the right was bred into them.

Before he'd tried that tack, she might've felt a little sympathy for his plight and perhaps would've been inclined to accept payment for his pa's ring. For the fact was that bloody ring was proving impossible to sell.

None of the pawnbrokers in the East End would touch it. *Too fine*, they all said. And none of the jewelers in the West End would deal with her once she opened her mouth and they heard the Cockney pouring out. A Cockney chit shouldn't be holding a ring like that. *Must be stolen*, they all thought. And there was the bottom of it—no one was willing to stick their neck out for a ring belonging to a nob. A real conundrum, this ring had proven itself.

Put another way, this wastrel lord crowding her cab bench with his broad shoulders and thick thighs and too handsome face might've been the answer to her prayers.

Then he'd gone and tried to bully her.

And the thing was this: these last nine years, no one had bullied Tilly Birdwell.

And she'd liked it that way.

So, she wasn't going to make it easy on him.

"It's the ring of an earl, you say?" she asked, all breezy like. That way, he wouldn't see her coming.

He exhaled in a great rush. "His signet, yes."

Didn't this too-handsome lord just brim with impatience?

Well, Tilly wouldn't be hurried. "So, it's a noble ring."

He searched her eyes, clearly trying to parse where she was going with this. "Aye."

"And how did you lose it again?" Toying with a lord was *fun*, wasn't it? "The first time, that is."

He hesitated, his eyes gone suspicious. "In a card game."

"You lost it *ignobly*, then?"

"If you want to put it that way."

Now, now, wasn't that a sore spot she'd touched?

She gave a little one-shouldered shrug that brushed along his arm. "Then there's one way you'll be getting the ring back."

The scowl trenched across his forehead said he didn't much trust either her words or the cheery way she'd spoken them. "And how's that?"

She spread her hands wide, like she'd seen magicians on the street do when they revealed their final trick. "You'll have to earn it…" Oh, how she liked making him wait for her next word… "*Nobly*."

That frown line would become permanent if he wasn't careful. "Pardon?"

Her smile couldn't contain itself. "If you do three noble deeds, I'll hand your pa's fancy ring over."

His mouth opened, then closed.

Her offer had clearly knocked him speechless.

"Three noble deeds, milord," she repeated in case she hadn't already made herself perfectly clear.

In the general sense, lords had trouble absorbing what they didn't want to hear.

Given his silence, Tilly felt she had leave to go on…

"You see, there's something I've always wondered. Why are aristocrats called *nobility*?"

A few seconds of silence ticked past before he came to and realized she'd asked a question—and expected an answer. "Never thought about it."

That got a good laugh out of her. "*You* wouldn't now, would you?"

His jaw tensed and released. "Fair play."

"And here's the thing," she continued, "in my experience of noblemen, I've only ever seen a few being noble."

His brow lifted, dry humor glinting in eyes that were more silver than blue. "Even a few?"

All right, he'd started playing along with her, but for some reason, it left a slick of sour in her mouth. This lord needed a few life lessons. "Do you know Lord Percival Bretagne?"

Of course, he would.

All nobs knew each other.

He shrugged. Now it was his shoulder brushing hers, and, *lawks*, there were more than a few muscles beneath that greatcoat of his. "Can anyone really know a man like Bretagne?" he asked. "If the rules aren't of his making, he feels no obligation to play by them."

Tilly took his meaning, but she also understood Isabel knew her husband, through and through, and had experienced naught but good from him. And that good in Lord Percival, Tilly had been the recipient of it, too. So, she had something to say to this lord and was feeling a mite righteous about it. "Lord Percival was the Savior of St. Giles, did you know that?"

His brow lifted a scant mite. "I didn't."

"*There*," she said, sure as a barrister. "*There* was a nobleman being noble when he shut down all them dens of iniquity."

The thing was, it wasn't only Isabel who had saved Tilly nine years ago. Lord Percival had been there that night, too.

The lord crammed at her side snorted. "I don't see myself becoming the Savior of St. Giles."

"Well, I wouldn't recommend losing any sleep over it," she said, all het up. "Not many men, noble or otherwise, can be Lord Percival Bretagne." She'd picked up on how the world saw Lord Percival—and she knew the world was dead wrong about him. He was loyal and true and *noble*. "And there's Hope House, too," she continued, unable not to now that she'd got going, "that he established to help all the doxies what wanted out of the life. Those women learn skills there that help them out in the world. Their sprigs, too."

If a snort could be sardonic, this lord's was. "A real paragon of virtue, that Lord Percival."

"But he's not a paragon." Here was what Tilly had been working up to say. "That's the point. He's a man. One doesn't need to be a paragon to be a *good* man or a *noble* man."

The man beside her had gone silent, and Tilly saw with no small amount of satisfaction that, at last, her words had their intended effect and struck up a war behind his eyes. Finally, he said, "Three noble deeds?"

She nodded, attempting not to let her surprise show.

She'd expected him to keep trying to bully her. But that look in his eyes communicated something different as he extended his hand. She took it and gave it a shake. "Three noble deeds," she said, her courage of a sudden turning into bravado.

It was his hand.

The feel of it, specifically—*big, strong, masculine*. Even through his gloves and her gloves, *warm*. A hand full of capability and strength.

It wasn't simply knowledge of those sensations—but awareness of them.

A shiver traced through her.

Nine years it had been since she was alone with a man who was touching her.

She'd made sure of it.

She even expected the little animal being who lived inside her to scream, *Run!*

But it didn't.

Another surprise, that.

The cab began to slow, and Tilly startled back into the present and snatched her hand back. A quick glance out the window told her they'd reached her first destination, Old Bond Street. She cleared her throat and clutched her reticule, any excuse to avoid his eyes. True silver, that was their color. Not a clear silver, but opaque with dark gray ringing the irises.

Those eyes should've been cold, but they weren't.

Neither were they warm.

Yet heat burned within.

The sort of heat that could burn straight through a woman, if she wasn't careful.

Lawks, this lord was a dead knocker, wasn't he?

This wasn't his first time sharing a carriage with a woman, either, for the instant the vehicle stopped, he edged past her—this carriage truly wasn't big enough for the two of them—and opened the door before jumping down to the cobbles, his hand extended to help her descend. It was the rare occasion that Tilly felt like a lady, but the feeling stole through her as she allowed those long, masculine fingers to take her hand—and there was that strength and warmth and capability.

Feet solidly on the ground, she reclaimed her hand and said, firm, like a lady would, "I have business to attend to."

With that, she brushed past him.

Heavy footsteps thudded behind her. She exhaled a sigh that implored the universe for patience, then swiveled around. "Don't you have a day to get on with?"

"We have yet a few matters to get straight between us," he said, as if the universe had granted *him* all the patience she'd asked for. "I still don't even know your name."

She saw two things at once.

Determination in his eyes—and the fact that he was right.

Perhaps she could give him her name, and he would be on his way.

Likely not.

"You can wait for me *here*." She indicated the patch of sidewalk beneath his feet. "I'll be out in ten minutes."

But as she entered Mrs. Marlow's Millinery, she heard

now-familiar footsteps following. Did the deuced man think she was looking to escape through the alley?

She shook him from her mind—or, more like, attempted to—and set about her business. She liked this millinery. Mrs. Marlow and her girls didn't put on any airs, and they had a genuine understanding of the vital functions a hat must perform all at once.

First off, for many a society lady, a hat was about propriety. Sometimes, it was about protection from the elements, like sun or rain. Those were the practicalities of a hat. But a *perfect* hat also needed to convey a lady's sense of style to the world. And topmost of all, as went a perfect hat: it must flatter, drawing the eye toward and away as one preferred.

"Tilly!" a voice rang out.

One of the girls—Maude—waved from her place behind a large rectangular table stacked with hatboxes waiting to be picked up. "I was just saying—" Her gaze shifted over Tilly's shoulder, and the words stopped dead in her mouth.

The lord in the shop had been spotted.

Well, he was hard to miss.

Another girl rushed forward, a greeting on her lips... That stopped dead, too.

Then, as suddenly, the shop went all aflutter. Seeing as how the place was empty of customers other than Tilly, its cause could've been precipitated by none other than that too-handsome lord.

The most handsome lord Tilly had personally beheld, she could allow.

Lawks.

Usually, she stayed for a while, taking her time to peruse various ribbons and trimmings. She liked to keep up-to-date about the newest products. Today, however, her business needed to reach its conclusion *posthaste*.

She needed to get rid of this lord.

She was tempted to give him the ring.

An idea she rejected for one reason alone.

This too-handsome, wastrel lord needed to learn something about life, and she supposed she was the one who was going to teach him.

And even if he learned nothing about life, he would learn something about *her*.

She wouldn't be bullied.

"Now," she said, firmly but kindly to the yet awestruck Maude, whose plainly infatuated gaze kept flicking over Tilly's shoulder, "let's take a look at this *chapeau femme*."

She liked using the French word for *hat*.

Everything sounded better in French.

Tilly's words seemed to break whatever spell that wastrel, rake lord held over Maude, and she set to the business of locating the correct hat box and prising the lid off. Carefully, Tilly lifted the hat and held it to the light pouring through the front window. "The color is perfect." That saffron yellow would bring out the vibrant green of Isabel's eyes. "And I do like this bit of lace…" She turned the hat. "But perhaps a more delicate netting would suit it better?" There was nothing worse than an overdecorated hat to overwhelm a lady. "Look here." She pointed. "Trim along *this* line all the way to the back, then instead of letting it drape, tuck it under and sew it in."

Maude nodded along, soaking up every word.

"And do you have any pheasant feathers in?"

"Aye."

"Put one here—" Again, she pointed to the precise placement. "And how dashing will Lady Percival look at that house party?"

"Oh, yes, Tilly, that's it." Maude smiled as she reclaimed the hat.

"Can you have it ready the day after tomorrow?"

The girl nodded. "I'll start on it right away."

Tilly could've, in fact, taken the hat and altered it herself—she had an entire cabinet full of supplies—but then Maude would never learn anything, would she? She would never know the pleasure and accomplishment of getting something just perfect for a client.

Tilly's sense of rightness in the world was short-lived, for she'd remembered something.

A man was in this shop with her—a *lord*.

She turned subtly, enough to locate him from the periphery of her vision. There, at the edge of her eye, stood his large, still form.

He'd been observing her exchange with Maude.

Unable not to, Tilly half twisted and met his gaze directly.

He didn't flinch.

Sudden and unexpected, she felt aflutter and observed and...oddly exposed.

That awareness she'd experienced in the carriage when

they'd shaken hands yet pulled an invisible thread between them…tethering them.

"Will that be all for you today, Tilly?" asked Maude.

She snapped to and tore her gaze from that man. What sort of spells was this wastrel lord capable of casting upon the female sex, anyway? With a light clearing of her throat, she turned toward Maude. "Got any new ribbons in?"

"Oh, yes," said the girl, brightening as she reached beneath the table. A few seconds later, several spools of ribbon of various colors and fabrics were strewn across the smooth pine surface.

Tilly didn't have much use for ribbons herself, but they would be the perfect gift for Miss Lavinia Asquith, who was the second cousin of Miss Lucy Bretagne, Lord Percival's daughter from his first marriage and Isabel's stepdaughter. Tilly knew she wasn't on the hook to buy all these folk Christmas gifts, but she liked doing it. She liked giving a gift and sparking that joy in a person's eyes when they knew they'd been thought of.

Anyway, Miss Asquith was a horsey sort, and a pink satin ribbon would look lovely fluttering in the breeze behind her as she rode.

While she was at it, Tilly also purchased a few yards of gold grosgrain that would make festive decoration in the drawing room in the lead-up to Christmas Eve and Day.

Then, she was speaking her farewells and exiting the shop, fully aware of the wastrel lord at her heels, as she made for Burlington Arcade, which was a few blocks away. In a matter of seconds, he was walking abreast with her and shooting her sideways glances. The man had something to say. But as with every man she'd ever met, her lack of prompting wouldn't stop him from saying it.

It only took him a few more steps. "Most people don't behave that way when their purchase is wrong."

She didn't know what words she'd expected him to speak, but they wouldn't have been those. "Well, I believe in second chances in this old life."

"So, your name is Tilly?"

She almost said *yes*.

Tilly was her name, after all.

Everyone called her Tilly.

But with this man—this handsome, wastrel lord—she might consider exercising a bit of cautious wisdom and establish a more formal relationship from the jump.

In fact, that was definitely the course of cautious wisdom.

"You can call me Miss Birdwell."

He nodded, taking in both what she'd said—and what she'd left unsaid. But that was a rule in the haut ton, wasn't it? In his world, a gentleman didn't call a lady by her given name—even if that lady was a mere woman.

A satisfied smile tickled about her mouth. It felt right nice to turn a rule around on a lord.

"Can I ask you another question?"

"You can certainly ask."

"Why were you in front of the Duke of Arundel's manse today?"

She saw no reason not to tell him at this point. "I'm Lady Percival's lady's maid, aren't I?"

"So, you're employed by Lord Percival, then."

"*Lady* Percival is who I answer to."

He nodded as if she'd confirmed something for him, and Tilly felt her satisfied smile slip and a little knot form in her stomach. This game wasn't feeling so very fun anymore, for she could tell this nob hadn't finished with his questions yet.

They'd rounded the corner onto Piccadilly when he asked, "How did you come by an invitation to the masquerade?"

Really, she should have seen the question coming. A surge of outrage had her exclaiming, "What's this about?" She was attracting no few askance glances from their fellow pedestrians, but she had no care, for she was good and het up. "You couldn't bully me, so now you're aiming to get me sacked?" She didn't wait for his response. "Because I'll have you know what me and Lady Percival have between us is loyalty, and some wastrel rake lord ain't going to get between us."

Silver-gray eyes wide, he lifted both hands, palms out, as if he were attempting to soothe a bristling cat. "That is not my intention."

Strangely, she believed him.

It wasn't just the gesture, but the look in his eyes, too.

This son of an earl might've been a wastrel and a rake, but he might've been an honest wastrel and rake.

Interesting, that.

She realized she was facing him like an adversary. So, while she was looking him in the eye, she took the opportunity to ask, "And what's *your* name?"

He didn't hesitate. "Lord Rhys Osborne," he said with a slight bow.

Mollified somewhat, she nodded, then started walking again.

"Where are we off to next?"

Lord Rhys looked like he expected an answer.

The bloody cheek of this man!

Tilly picked up her pace, her boot heels a sharp *click-clack* against cobblestones. Heat in both her step and her voice, she tossed over her shoulder, "*We* aren't off to anywhere next."

6

The thing was, Rhys didn't have a day he was particularly keen to get on with.

For he'd found that the day he wanted to have, well, he was having it.

Except...he now had in his possession all the information he needed to start moving forward and earning Papa's ring back.

He knew the blonde's name—*Miss Tilly Birdwell.*

He knew for whom she worked—*Lady Percival Bretagne*—and, by extension, where she lived, for a lady's maid lived in the household of her employer.

Strictly speaking, no more facts were required for him to be able to send a note informing her of his noble deeds.

He could part ways with this woman right here on this stretch of Piccadilly sidewalk.

But he found he didn't want to part ways with her.

Simply, there was something about Miss Tilly Birdwell.

And, *nay*, it wasn't her looks or her figure or her appeal to both eyes and other parts of the body.

Well, it wasn't *only* that.

It was *her*.

This woman held a light inside her.

As someone who had spent the last year in the dark—and the ten preceding that, frankly—he wanted to bask in that light a little and perhaps understand it some.

She came to a sudden stop before a shop—The Pantheon of Play. His eyebrows winged together. "You're shopping at a toy store?"

Miss Birdwell tilted her head to the side, observing him from a distance that allowed for the possibility that he'd gone daft. "It's the Christmas season, ain't it?"

His brow gathered. "You mean, *December*?"

Her head tipped to the other side. "You don't celebrate Christmas?"

"My family gathers for Christmas Eve supper, if that's what you're asking."

Her mouth turned down at the corners. "No gifts, then?"

Discomfort traced through Rhys. "My family believes gifts are for the—" He couldn't finish that sentence, of course.

Miss Birdwell heard it anyway, and instead of taking offense, a laugh sprang from her. "Gifts are for us vulgar *lower* classes, innit?" Even as her smile teased, her eyes looked inclined to take pity on him. "It's all right, Lord Rhys. I'm a servant in a grand household, and I've heard worse from your lot."

A surprising urge to defend reared up inside him. "Do Lord and Lady Percival not treat you—"

Miss Birdwell reached out and did the most surprising thing: she placed a calming hand on his arm. "Not them. Lord Percival and Isabel are the best of the best. And his pa the duke is, too, along with the duchess. Now, the duke's heir and his wife, Lord and Lady Exeter, who live in the west wing of the house, they have a way of thinking about us of lower consequence that can come out in their words every so often."

Ah.

Now Rhys knew something more about Miss Birdwell.

She was a tactful, forgiving sort. He'd met Lord and Lady Exeter on a few occasions, and they likely weren't deserving of such grace.

"Now," said Miss Birdwell, pushing the shop door open, "let's buy some toys."

Let's buy some toys.

It wasn't the *buying of toys* part that lit a spark of excitement inside him, but the *let's* part.

No longer was she attempting to exclude him from her day.

He'd become part of it.

After Miss Birdwell had exchanged greetings with the shopkeeper, Rhys asked, "Who are these children you're buying gifts for? I wasn't aware that Lord and Lady Percival have any."

"Well, the good Lord hasn't seen fit to bless them with sprigs," said Miss Birdwell, "but we have lots of little ones in our circle. There's Miss Bretagne from Lord Percival's first marriage, but she's a lady full-grown now, isn't she? But then, Miss Bretagne has the twin brothers from her mam's second marriage, so they're part of the circle. Then Miss Bretagne has cousins on her mam's side, Miss Lavinia Asquith and Mr. Geoffrey Asquith—also twins, mind you —though they're grown, too, which ain't to say they wouldn't want gifts, y'know?"

Rhys nodded, not exactly *knowing*. "I suppose."

"Then there's other cousins, too. The French ones from Isabel's sister, Eva, who is a French aristocrat now, and has three sprigs of her own."

Rhys had yet another question, and he needed to ask it delicately, for he didn't wish to offend. "So, all these gifts are for the family of your employers?"

Miss Birdwell brightened. "Oh, and my friend Nell, who is a duchess now and has her own two sprigs."

Rhys found himself nodding again. "And Nell's sprigs."

"Family comes in all forms, don't it?"

Against his will and whatever sound judgment he possessed—which, admittedly, had always been in short supply—Rhys was impressed by this woman.

There was no artifice to her.

"That's quite a lot of people to buy for," he said, neutrally.

Her smile turned brilliant. "Isn't it wonderful?"

That hadn't precisely been his point, but he saw hers— and liked it better.

A lot of people to buy for was a wonderful thing in her world.

And so it was, one hour later, Rhys was stepping

outside the Pantheon of Play weighed down by six boxes of varying sizes. Felt more like juggling.

Miss Birdwell gave him an up-and-down appraisal and laughed. "That doesn't count as one of your three noble deeds, so don't go getting any ideas."

A low, rumbly chuckle of his own joined hers. He'd never met a woman like her. This woman's angle on life was different from anyone's he'd ever known.

"Now," she said, pointing across the covered walkway of Burlington Arcade, "I need to pop into that silversmith's shop for a dog collar for Miss Bretagne—"

"A dog collar for Miss Bretagne?"

"Not *for* her," said Miss Birdwell, still smiling. "For the spaniel puppy she's getting for Christmas."

"Ah, that makes more sense."

Another laugh escaped Miss Birdwell. "Wouldn't she just make a sight showing up to one of them fancy balls wearing a dog collar?"

While she "popped in" to the silversmith's, then the goldsmith's beside it—"for a pair of earbobs for Isabel"— Rhys continued holding the boxes of toys and waiting. As Burlington Arcade was frequented by the haut ton, he was recognized by a few passersby—a nod from the gents…a quick cut of the eye, followed by a private little smile from the ladies. But as Burlington Arcade was mostly frequented by the proper end of society, he wasn't on conversational terms with any of them.

Those of the *ton* with whom he was on conversational terms tended to occupy the opposite end of the spectrum— the wastrels, rotters, and tossers.

When Miss Birdwell returned, she was holding two small boxes and her smile, which he'd come to understand was just how she always looked—which he more than liked.

Some place inside him responded to her smile.

And he understood.

He couldn't pack her and her boxes into a hackney cab and end this day.

He thoroughly wracked his brain until a simple, perfect solution came to him. "Shall we have tea?"

"*Tea?*" Her brow crinkled, and her smile faltered. She looked as if she didn't know how to interpret the suggestion. "With *you?*"

"Why not with me?"

"Well, you're a…"

"A *lord?*"

"Well…" She shrugged one shoulder.

"Please don't hold that against me," he said, trying for lightness, but underneath sincerely earnest. "I promise I don't bite."

Unless you ask, he didn't say.

Didn't even know where that came from.

Well, that wasn't precisely true.

It had come from the rake that, plainly, wouldn't mind having his way with the delectable bit of sweet that was this Miss Birdwell. He'd become decently skilled at suppressing his inner rake this last year. But here he was, suddenly desperate for a private hour with this woman— even fifteen minutes would do in a pinch.

Head tipped to the side, Miss Birdwell considered him

with her little smile. "And where do you propose we take tea?"

"Mivart's, of course."

Her eyebrows made a break for Burlington Arcade's vaulted glass ceiling. "*Mivart's?*"

"It's no more than a few streets away."

"You're all right to carry them boxes all that way?"

"Bracing exercise."

She gave a little shrug and started walking, but almost as quickly stopped in her tracks before a mullioned window. "Oh."

"What is it?"

"It's vacant."

"Was this shop a favorite of yours?"

She shook her head and waved his question away. "Wouldn't it be something to have a shop in *the* Burlington Arcade?"

Rhys understood there were a great many unanswered questions floating around in the ether that he'd never once pondered—and this was one of them. "Hmm."

Miss Birdwell hardly noticed his response—or lack thereof. "It's the perfect location for a shop for ladies."

"Why for ladies?" he asked, wondering if he'd missed something—*likely*. "Don't ladies shop everywhere?"

Incredulous blue eyes rounded on him. "*For* ladies."

As if that cleared anything up.

But he nodded, anyway.

She pointed down the long stretch of the arcade. "You've got all these shops here. Then beyond, you've got Piccadilly." She pointed the opposite direction. "You've got

Old Bond Street." She pointed yet another direction. "Then New Bond Street. So many milliners, dressmakers, shoemakers, and jewelers all around."

He didn't know how to react in the face of all her passion.

And that was…*new*.

His past self—and his present self, to be honest—knew exactly how to handle a woman's passion…inside a bed.

But never had he encountered this level of passion outside it.

Well, he *had*.

The sort of passion that involved beds could be had as easily outside it.

But the passion of Miss Tilly Birdwell was a different sort altogether.

Her eyes burned with the fervor of a Renaissance saint, as she said, "An entrepreneurial spirit could make something of it." Then she snorted and shook her head. "A gel like me couldn't have a shop here."

"Why not?"

"*You* would ask that, wouldn't you?"

"*Me?*"

"A lord."

He supposed he would never live that condition down.

He would always be a lord.

Then they were walking in earnest, traversing the blocks between them and a luxurious tea in silence, and it occurred to Rhys that, perhaps, he should've offered to take her to Gunter's instead of Mivart's.

Mivart's was one of London's premiere hotels, and as such, it was fashionable and exclusive.

It also happened to have been a place where he'd met more than a few ladies for an indiscreet *tête-à-tête*.

Well, today his intentions were pure as the driven snow.

He simply wanted to take Miss Birdwell there for tea.

Treat her to it.

This woman, who was a lady's maid and sometime card cheat and indiscriminate giver of Christmas gifts and possessor of passions great, she deserved a treat.

The doorman, having recognized Rhys from rakish days past, readily swung the front door wide for them with a wink. Then it was the concierge rushing forward. "Lord Rhys, it has been a while."

He nodded in greeting. "A table for two for tea."

Discreetly, but not imperceptibly, the concierge appraised Miss Birdwell and would've immediately determined Lord Rhys Osborne was accompanied by a woman who wasn't a lady. So, he led them through the mostly empty banquet room used for afternoon tea service and seated them at a discreet corner table.

Miss Birdwell wouldn't have noticed.

But Rhys did.

And he was irritated.

Irritated by the quiet class snobbery.

Irritated, even, that Miss Birdwell didn't notice.

Or, worse, she'd noticed, but didn't care.

None of which he would mention and spoil her fun.

Besides, perhaps she had the right end of the stick, and he the wrong.

In fact, that was very likely the case.

Once they were seated, they faced each other across the table with, apparently, not a single thing to say.

"So," she said.

"So," he replied.

"You're the sprig of an earl."

"I am."

"But not the heir."

"No."

"The spare, then."

"Not even the spare, I'm afraid. I am a third son." He snorted. "The entirely useless sort of son."

"The third son of an *earl*."

"A minor earl."

Her head canted, and, at last, there was her smile again. "Are there minor earls?"

"Fair play."

Her eyes narrowed. "You're not entirely useless, though, are you?"

"Maybe not *entirely*, but…" *It was a near thing*, he didn't need to say.

"You don't mind everyone thinking so, do you?"

"Not particularly."

She nodded. "That way no one has expectations. But…"

"*But?*"

She shook her head and settled back in her chair. "It's not my place to say."

Rhys sat forward, his elbows coming to rest on the table. "Say it."

"To my way of thinking," she said, "isn't it good to carry some expectations on your shoulders? Because when someone puts expectations on you, it means something."

"It does?"

"It means someone thinks highly enough of you to reckon you could live up to those expectations. That they believe in you."

He'd never thought of it like that.

This woman… What a revelation she was.

She shrugged a shoulder. "Anyway, that's what I think, and not too many folk give a sod about *that*." She laughed.

But Rhys didn't find himself laughing along with her. "*I care what you think.*"

And he found it wasn't just words.

It was the truth.

Opaque emotion passed behind her eyes, clouding their clear blue. "I think…" she began, "I think if you knew anything about me, you wouldn't."

The servers arrived to lay the table and serve tea, so Rhys settled back in his chair and gave them room—and considered Miss Birdwell.

I think if you knew anything about me, you wouldn't.

She had a past.

That was what she was saying.

She was also saying she wouldn't be sharing it with him.

Well, if she didn't want to talk about her past, then the present would have to do. He waited for the servers to clear out before he said, "You're quite skilled at your work, it appears."

She dropped a lump of sugar into her tea, followed by a dollop of cream. "Oh, it's hardly work when you're good at something and love it."

A sudden chord of envy struck through Rhys. What she was describing… He'd never felt that once in his life. He couldn't even say he loved being a wastrel rake. He'd been good at it, certainly, but it had been more compulsion than love that drove it.

Especially as the years passed and began bleeding into one another.

"I was good at being a wastrel rake."

She finished stirring her tea, then canted her head, a little mischievous smile playing about her mouth. "You speak like you aren't still a wastrel rake."

Touché, he supposed.

After all, she did first meet him at a card table at a masquerade ball.

But there was something he needed to say, aloud to another person, rather than only to himself. "I'm not a wastrel rake." He added, "Anymore, that is."

"How's that?"

"When I lost the ring to Sir Felix a year ago, that was my low point. I had to change my ways."

"That's why you were at the masquerade, then."

He nodded. "To expose Sir Felix and get Papa's ring back."

Her mouth formed an O as she blew across the surface of her tea, and Rhys found his eyes lingering a beat too long on those lovely plump lips of hers. Her throat cleared, and his gaze startled up to meets hers, watching him.

He'd been caught out staring—and didn't mind one bit.

That rake yet took up residence inside him, didn't he?

"But you didn't count on me." Her eyes sparkled like blue topazes and her mouth curved into that mischievous smile never too far away and she laughed.

That night, the moment she'd won the ring had been one of the worst of his life. Yet now, he found his mouth smiling along with hers and a laugh of his own joining hers, too.

Strangely, the more he laughed…the more he laughed. As if an avalanche of laughter had been unleashed inside him that felt nothing less than soul-clearing.

Soul-clearing.

His soul craved this laughter, like a parched throat craved water in the desert. They were likely being inappropriate and causing a scene, but he didn't care.

And this laughter, he understood, would be sparked by this woman—and shared with her.

He found he liked sharing with her.

People took life so seriously, and life *was* serious, which was why laughter was so necessary.

All those years he'd spent playing the wastrel rake, he'd thought he'd been laughing at the *ton*, at the world.

But he hadn't, had he?

He'd been a drowning man.

But *this* laughter, shared with *this* woman, it was buoyant.

It lifted him up.

He could easily become addicted to it.

And the thought struck him that perhaps he already was.

Like an opium eater's first hit of the pipe, perhaps that was what laughter shared with this woman was.

And it occurred to him.

At the end of this tea, he couldn't simply let her walk out of his life.

Well, she wouldn't be, precisely.

The ring still bound them.

And the three noble deeds.

The ring...the three noble deeds...

A chord of inspiration struck him. "About our terms for the ring."

She exhaled the last of her laughter, a glint of suspicion replacing it in her eyes. "What of them?"

"The three noble deeds."

"Was this—" She swept her arm around their luxurious surroundings. "Was this all about sweetening me up so I'd just hand over your pa's ring?"

He'd miscalculated his approach—and needed to right this ship before it veered irretrievably off course. "How will you know?"

"How will I know *what*?"

"That I've held up my end of the bargain and actually done my noble deeds."

Understanding lit within her eyes. "Ah."

"I mean, how can you trust me?" asked Rhys, pressing his point home. "I'm a known wastrel and rake."

"I thought you said you were on the mend."

"You only have my word that I'm reformed. In my heart, I could be entirely and unapologetically *unreformed*."

"That so?"

He spread his hands wide. "So, I have a solution."

"What's that?"

"You must witness my noble deeds."

Miraculously, his rakish, wastrel past was of use to him here, for he'd not only turned their bargain a hair to his advantage, he'd given himself some of the whip hand, too.

And—as if that wasn't enough—he would now get to spend more time with Miss Birdwell and her interesting perspective on life and her buoyancy of the soul.

At last, she nodded. "All right."

The triumph that sheered through him was surely too exaggerated for the accomplishment.

But it didn't feel that way.

It felt like the first good thing to have happened to him in years.

"When's your next day off?" He didn't plan on dragging his anchor.

"I don't really take days off."

"When do you have time to yourself?" He felt his brow furrow. "When do you have fun?"

"That's not how I look at life."

"Then how do you look at it?" He genuinely wanted to know.

"Every day and every moment of the life I live now is better than the one that came before it."

It wasn't that she'd uttered some earth-shattering, awe-inducing statement, but rather her words were the opposite.

They were simple and humble and struck a place inside Rhys that knew the truth when he heard it.

She reached for her reticule and sat it on her lap, a none-too-subtle indicator that their tea was nearing its end. "How about you send me a note with the date and time for your first noble deed, and I'll be there. Then soon enough, you'll never have to see me again."

Rhys froze.

You'll never have to see me again.

He didn't like the sound of that—the finality.

Instinctively, his best charming smile found its way to his mouth—the very smile the rake in him had spent years refining—and he said in a low, crushed-velvet voice, "Didn't you enjoy our afternoon together, Miss Birdwell?"

An ineffable something flickered behind her eyes, and her mouth twitched as if it wanted to smile, but caught itself.

Ground gained…ground lost.

"I did," she said as primly as a woman like her could.

Women like her fancied a little frivolous flirting.

And Rhys had always taken great pleasure in flirting.

So, here they were—*flirting.*

Which was why he asked, "Now, why wouldn't you want to see me again?"

Oh, his unreformed self was reveling in the light, wasn't he?

The rake that needed to be desired by every woman whose eyes happened across him.

She gave a little, feminine laugh. "Because you're a sort."

"A *sort*?"

He knew what sort, but he wanted to hear her say it.

Another laugh along with a shake of her head. "Oh, you're definitely a sort, Lord Rhys."

He found himself laughing along with her, improbably. "And what sort is that?"

"The love-'em-'til-morning-and-leave-'em sort."

"And who doesn't like to be loved until morning?" He held her gaze. "I suspect *you*, Miss Birdwell, are very much that sort."

Like that, she froze, and her laughter fell away—as if he'd doused the conversation with a bucket of ice water. "Well, Lord Rhys, you don't really know the first thing about me."

She stood, awkwardly, indicating both tea and their conversation were at an end.

As they made their way out of Mivart's, him hauling her boxes of toys and her holding onto her silence, he understood something.

He wanted to know more about her—and he would.

That desire had already become determination as he deposited her and her packages into a waiting hackney cab, paid the driver, and watched it roll away.

Already, he missed this woman he'd only known for a handful of hours.

This woman who was buoyant light personified.

But he would see her again.

That was the main thing.

She wasn't out of his life.

She'd even given him an idea for his first noble deed.

"Not many men, noble or otherwise, can be Lord Percival Bretagne."

She'd told him not to lose any sleep over the fact.

He felt like he'd been dealt the backhand of an insult, for the implication was clear: *he* wasn't a man who could be like Lord Percival Bretagne.

A man Miss Birdwell clearly admired.

And if Rhys was the opposite of Lord Percival, then another implication was clear, too.

He wasn't the sort of man Miss Birdwell could admire.

He liked that even less.

Though hardly any time had passed since she'd spoken those words to him, he already felt haunted by them and that implication.

He was going to lose sleep over it.

But the day wasn't all bad.

He had a path to recovering Papa's ring.

And he saw another path, too, one that ran alongside it.

A path toward earning Miss Birdwell's respect.

A path he just thought he would pursue.

7

JANE STREET, LONDON, FOUR DAYS LATER

Tilly alighted from the hired hackney cab, faced the plain, red-brick exterior of Hope House, and not for the first time, experienced a smattering of surprise at finding herself here.

Well, not surprise at finding herself at Hope House in general.

She'd been here before to lend a helping hand. Several times, in fact.

Today, however, she wasn't here to offer help.

She was here to observe.

That was what had her surprised.

The reason for her presence here—in the specific.

The first surprise had been that the letter had come at all.

But yesterday, there it had been in tidy black and white —Lord Rhys Osborne requesting her presence at Hope House at two in the afternoon to bear witness to his first noble deed.

Until then, she'd figured Lord Rhys wasn't as reformed as he claimed and would deem the price for getting his pa's ring back too high.

That was the conclusion most lordly wasters would have reached. Most lords, the wasters and the righteous alike, didn't appreciate having to work for that which they wanted.

In fact, Tilly hadn't believed those black-and-white words the first time she'd read them.

The second pass hadn't yielded much more belief.

Upon the third read, those words finally communicated themselves as fact.

And with that acceptance came a feeling.

A light, little feeling that whissed through her that she thought it best not to examine closely.

The thing was, she'd come away from her afternoon with Lord Rhys Osborne with an altogether different feeling from the one that had begun it.

By the end, she'd been enjoying it.

There.

She'd enjoyed herself.

A few reasons why presented themselves.

First, she wasn't so above the superficialities not to take a measure of delight from having the upper hand over the handsome son of an earl.

Well, once he realized he couldn't bully her.

Or had he tried to bully her?

Upon reflection, she didn't think so.

Also, he hadn't tried it on with her.

That was new.

Most men of a type took one look at Tilly Birdwell and made up their minds to add her to their stable of female conquests.

Or to, at least, try.

They discovered right quick the error in their thinking.

But Lord Rhys… His eyes had shown his attraction, and he'd flirted a little, but he hadn't seriously pursued a dalliance.

He'd treated her like someone he was interested in—not as someone to be seduced and discarded.

It had allowed her to relax and enjoy her fancy tea at Mivart's.

A suspicion had entered her mind regarding Lord Rhys Osborne.

That he might not be like most lords.

That he might have a good heart.

But he didn't seem all that acquainted with that part of himself, as the necessity to use it had likely never presented itself.

This was the case for most lords and ladies.

They built up a world of luxury around themselves so they never had to experience a genuine feeling in all their lives.

They never had to use their hearts.

After all, things like hearts and real feelings could be inconvenient, and if there was one thing aristocrats didn't like, it was being inconvenienced.

Lord Rhys, it surprised her to think, might not be like that.

Of course, she'd been wrong about lords before.

But then she'd been sixteen, and Sir Felix had been an accomplished deceiver.

Now that was something she and Lord Rhys had in common, wasn't it? They'd both been on the deceived end when it came to their dealings with Sir Felix Mortimer.

She entered the front door of Hope House, and her feet stuttered to an immediate stop. Usually, Hope House was a place of quiet and stillness—*calm*. Today, it sounded as if Bedlam itself had relocated within its four walls, so noisy and energetic was the air. A child with a gold bow affixed to the top of his head streaked past, a second boy charging fast on his heels. A sudden squeal of laughter erupted from the drawing room door they'd bounded through.

Actually, several squeals of laughter.

Tilly took a step in that direction to investigate—a suspicion of what or *who* might provoke such an atmosphere forming and firming in her mind in the same instant—when a voice sounded at her back, "Tilly, we have a visitor."

She twisted around to find Lucy had joined her in the foyer. Tilly supposed she should call the step-daughter of her employer Miss Bretagne, but she'd always called her Lucy. Lucy returned the favor by calling her Tilly. An arrangement that suited them both.

"What sort of visitor is that?" Though Tilly knew.

"A *male* one." That *male* held more than a hint of exasperation.

"Oh?"

"A *lord*, in fact."

"*Lawks*, fancy as all that?"

Lucy nodded, blonde curls bobbing, her lively light amber eyes sparkling with confounded amusement. "A few days ago, I received a letter from Lord Rhys Osborne, asking how he could be of use at Hope House." A dry laugh sounded through her nose. "I thought it must be a jape."

"Why's that?"

"Lord Rhys Osborne has a reputation." Lucy waggled her eyebrows for emphasis.

"Does he now?"

Tilly supposed he hadn't been exaggerating that past of his.

Lucy seemed only too happy to elaborate on the topic. "I've personally heard him described as a rake from a lady who, honestly, probably knows firsthand. Oh, and *unrepentant waster*. That was another description." She shook her head on a snort. "I thought he must be inveigling himself into Hope House to look for his favorite, *erm*, lady of the night. He does have a reputation, you know, so one must be forgiven for thinking as much."

"Cuts quite a figure in society then?"

Lucy's eyes rolled toward the ceiling. "Even with his reputation, half the ladies I know would run off with him at the slightest crook of his pinky."

From everything Tilly had observed of the man, that squared.

"A real paragon of manhood, it sounds like."

That got another snort from Lucy.

Yet there was something else Tilly felt she must say on the subject of Lord Rhys Osborne… "Maybe he's here trying to reform himself."

Or earn back his pa's ring, she wouldn't say.

Tilly found herself of two minds.

On one side, she itched to ask questions and get answers.

Plainly, she wanted to know more about Lord Rhys.

But Lucy knew him only by reputation.

Which, according to him, was the man he was a year ago.

The man he was trying to no longer be.

Which led Tilly to the other side of her mind.

That she should resist gossipy curiosity and come to know Lord Rhys as the person he was today.

That in doing so, she could allow him to be that person.

After all, nine years ago, wasn't that the grace Isabel had extended to *her*?

Shouldn't everyone get the opportunity at a second chance when they were really trying?

Unable to keep her curiosity at bay a moment longer, Tilly stepped into the drawing room's open doorway, the sight before her stopping her in her tracks.

"See what I mean?" said Lucy, her voice pitched low.

This was definitely a scene from Bedlam. Frenetic children running around and playing—some laughing…some squealing—while others sat still and quiet, half seated around the massive boat that could only be a Noah's Ark with all the attendant animals littered about and the other half gathered before the four-story dollhouse and the little people and furnishings. Meanwhile, the children's mothers were arranged on the sofas and adjacent armchairs, taking tea as if nothing out of the ordinary was happening in their day.

A scene straight out of Bedlam, yes, but also curiously magical.

And it was down to the man whose back was to them as he shuttled to and fro, obeying one command after the other from the women, whose eyes shone with equal parts mischief, appreciation, and delight. They were having a right grand old time, weren't they?

Tilly leaned toward Lucy. "Lord Rhys brought all this?"

Lucy nodded. "I think he meant well."

"How do you mean?"

"I'm not sure he fully understands the order of events as pertains to the giving of gifts to children for Christmas."

A smile tickled at the corner of Tilly's mouth.

That heart of Lord Rhys's… It was a good one, wasn't it?

"An hour ago, he turned up with the toys and wrapping paper." Lucy shook her head, thoroughly bemused. "It took at least five trips back and forth from his carriage to unload it all."

Tilly could see it would, given all the toys and decorations.

"I think he thought the children would help wrap the toys?" Lucy sounded unsure herself if she was asking a question or answering it. "It's a conundrum," she continued. "But then, the more I contemplate the man, I think Lord Rhys is a bit of a conundrum. Just look at him."

He was presently pouring tea for a trio of former doxies

who were clearly thrilled at having their own personal lord they could order around.

And not just any lord, but *this* lord.

Just look at him.

And weren't they all, just.

Tilly's giggle that wanted airing would be held back no longer and spilled over. Lucy joined her for a few chuckles, then was off.

Leaving Tilly with her laughter—and this priceless view.

She knew the instant her giggle reached Lord Rhys, for he went still, his head cocked. Then he turned, and Tilly had to suppress a gasp.

Just look at him.

During these four days she hadn't seen him, she'd almost had herself convinced he wasn't as handsome or magnetic as she'd left Mivart's thinking he was.

No man could be.

But Lord Rhys Osborne...*was.*

All that floppy black hair that curled at his collar. Those silver eyes. Those cheekbones. Those lips that were a little too beautifully formed for a man's mouth.

My, oh my, the havoc this man must've wreaked upon the female sex during his wastrel rake days.

And as his eyes held hers, Tilly experienced a frisson of heat and something else, too. Something that fizzed through her and awakened all her senses. Something that made her feel more alive than usual.

All that from simply meeting his gaze.

A smile curved one side of his mouth, and her breath caught in her lungs.

The effect of a smile from that man was no minor thing.

"Oi!" cried one of the women on the sofa.

Resignation to his fate replaced the humor in his eyes. Clearly, he knew that *oi!*

"Me teacup won't be refreshing itself," said a second woman. "And I have some butter and jam that need spreading, too."

That got a hearty round of laughter.

Tilly snorted and entered the room, but not to join the women for tea. Rather, she made her way to the dollhouse where several young girls were busy as bees arranging the tiny pieces of furniture inside the little rooms. "What do we have here?"

As she settled into the game of house with the girls, Tilly kept half an eye on Lord Rhys. Between the women and the children, he was being run ragged from one task to the next —serving tea…hanging decorations…extracting a toy giraffe whose long neck had become wedged inside the ark…

And she thought she might've been right about him.

She wasn't sure he was good in the narrow way folk associated with *good* men.

He didn't seem pious or particularly upright.

But he had good inside him—good intentions…a good heart.

The point was this Lord Rhys Osborne had no bad in him.

Which to her way of thinking counted for a lot.

How many *"good"* men had she known that were all bad on the inside?

"Oh, Lord Rhys?"

"Yeah?" he asked over his shoulder. Presently, he was on the top step of a stool in front of the hearth where he was hanging a gold star.

"This tea service won't march itself back to the kitchen and clean itself up."

From her place on the floor, Tilly watched his shoulders lift and fall. Then he said, "All right."

He placed the gold star on the mantle, unhung, as he set to the task assigned him, sparing a harassed glance for Tilly in the process.

Again, she giggled and immediately felt naughty for taking such delight in his travails—then giggled again.

He straightened with the tea tray. "Where is the kitchen?"

Tilly scrambled to her feet. "I'll show you."

They weren't three steps down the corridor when he groused, "I can't see how this disaster of a day will count as a noble deed."

"Oh, I don't know," said Tilly, all breezy in stark contrast to his plain frustration. "I rather think it does."

Black eyebrows made for the ceiling. "You do?"

"It's the intention behind a deed that makes it noble, innit?"

His brow furrowed, her words working on his frustration and wounded pride.

Again, she giggled, and the look of betrayal he shot her

only induced another giggle. "Oh, Lord Rhys, but you were outnumbered, and those women were determined to have their way with you and cause some mischief."

He snorted, and with the release returned that lightness she'd come to associate with this man. Half a smile curved his mouth, and he shook his head.

"A lord at the beck and call of a bevy of erstwhile strumpets?" she couldn't resist saying as they crossed the kitchen to the scullery, where the washing up happened. "I'd say you made their day. So, a noble deed, aye. Now," she continued, shrugging off her pelisse and draping it over the back of a chair, "have you ever washed a dish in your life?"

"I, *erm*, haven't."

A possibility struck her. "Have you ever even been in a kitchen?"

"Of course," he said, defensive, then added, "a few times."

As they stood, nearly shoulder to shoulder, her washing the dirty dishes in the soapy sink and him dipping them in the rinse sink, then placing the clean dishes on a towel to dry on the counter, she marveled. Housework with a lord... Couldn't this old world offer up some surprises?

Once he'd rinsed the last teacup and set it on the towel, he turned to face her. A question was about to be asked, and she braced for it.

"Why did you cheat Sir Felix at the masquerade?"

She should've figured he would ask at some point. "We had a history," she said tightly.

Lord Rhys's head cocked. The question within his eyes

remained, unsatisfied. "Do you get to know many lords like Sir Felix in your occupation as a lady's maid?"

Had a man ever asked a question with as much skepticism?

Tilly had a choice.

Lie—or tell the truth.

It was that simple—and that complex.

She supposed a third option lay open to her, too.

An option that had served her well in that complex past of hers.

Run, said the little animal being that lived inside her.

But her feet remained in place, for there was another being inside her, one recently born, in fact, that wanted to answer the question for a single reason—it was Lord Rhys asking it.

"I met Sir Felix in my previous occupation."

His brow wrinkled ever so subtly, and he looked as if he very much regretted having asked—as if she'd confirmed something he'd been wondering. "Miss Birdwell," he began, "please don't feel obligated to answer my questions if I'm being too forward—"

"I was fourteen." She'd interrupted him, because if she didn't, she was either going to lie or run and she didn't want to do either of those things. "Fourteen when life circumstances turned about and I became a strumpet."

"A strumpet at...*fourteen*?" But he wasn't truly asking. "*Life circumstances?*"

She allowed there was much to parse in that one sentence, so she reckoned she would help him out. "The lives of poor folk involve a lot of struggle and illness and death. An altogether different set of problems than your lot are accustomed to. So, by fourteen, me parents had both gone to meet their Maker and I found meself alone in the world without two pennies to rub together and two life options in front of me—Saint Mary Magdalen Workhouse or Pizzy's Pleasure Palace."

"Pizzy's Pleasure Palace?"

"Heard of it, have you?" She'd asked with a little meanness in her heart, truth told. "Perhaps from those wastrel days of yours?"

"It rings a bell." He didn't look inclined to say more.

And she didn't feel inclined to make him. "For various reasons, and mostly because I was young and uninformed, I chose Pizzy's." She spread hands helpless to the past wide. "And that was me a strumpet."

"At *fourteen*?" he repeated.

"I developed certain attributes deeply appreciated by men at an early age." Namely, her bounteous bosom.

Lord Rhys somehow managed to look both slightly red *and* slightly green and altogether like he might need to sit down.

But now that she'd started in on the past, she was determined to keep going. "After a couple of years"—a couple of years she had no intention of discussing—"Sir Felix came along." She shrugged. "He was handsome and a lord and he was everything my sixteen-year-old self ever dreamed of. A knight in shining armor who would rescue me. He made me those promises, and I believed them. But those promises were fool's gold, weren't they? You've been around, Lord Rhys, you can guess what came next."

His jaw tensed and released. "He abandoned you."

"Discarded after he'd wrung all the fun he wanted out of me and left me to rot as a poxy, old harlot in my dotage."

"Then how did you—"

"*Isabel.*" He didn't need to finish his question for her to answer it. "*She* was my knight in shining armor—and that was my lesson learned."

She'd said that last a little offhand, and from the darkening of Lord Rhys's brow she could see he didn't like her flippancy. "What lesson was that?"

"That one's dreams are precious, and they are one's own. You can't depend on another person to realize them."

He'd gone quiet as he listened and took in her words—her confession.

"And now, Miss Birdwell?" he asked. "Do you have new dreams that have taken the place of the old ones?"

Yes, she almost said, but held her tongue still.

A man like this lord couldn't understand the dreams of someone like her. Her dreams were pragmatic, not the lofty or high-minded ones born aristocrats could aim for. Her dreams flew closer to the ground.

What would this man—*lord*—understand of her dream to open a shop?

He'd never washed a single dish in his life until ten minutes ago.

She couldn't tell this man her dreams.

"Oh, Lord Rhys!" sing-songed a female East End voice from the other side of the house.

Relief pulsed through Tilly. "I believe your services are wanted."

"Oh, lord," he groaned, making her laugh, breaking the moment.

"Take heart, Lord Rhys," she said. "That's your first noble deed done."

His brow trenched deep into his forehead. "You're not leaving, are you?"

"I have a day to get on with, and I've witnessed enough." She began walking away. "Send me another note when it's time for your second noble deed," she tossed over her shoulder.

Then she was saying her farewells to Lucy and making her way out of Hope House and into a hackney cab, all accomplished with a light step, but a heavy thought in her mind.

The truth was she had the rest of the afternoon free.

But she'd had to leave.

Because if she'd stayed, it wouldn't have been to witness further noble deeds from Lord Rhys.

She would've been staying for *him*.

Which was an altogether different thing.

It was the sort of thing that could lead her down a path.

And she knew better than to follow paths involving handsome lords.

Even lords with good inside them.

Maybe especially those lords.

8

———

A WEEK LATER

Loose fist poised to knock on the kitchen door, Rhys just held off.

What was he thinking?

The short answer was he wasn't.

Actually, he had been thinking—and that was the problem.

Not the thinking itself, but the subject of it.

Miss Tilly Birdwell.

After several days of wracking his brain, he'd finally happened across an idea for his second noble deed somewhere in a far corner. The idea was so obvious he could've kicked himself for not having thought it sooner. Ever since, he'd been itching to tell Miss Birdwell—in person.

Any excuse to see her, really.

He understood that much.

And as a desperate mind was wont to do, it hatched another idea.

How easily he could deliver the details for his second

noble deed while she shared the evening meal in the kitchen with the other servants in the Bretagne household. Everyone had to eat, didn't they?

This afternoon, it had seemed like the perfect plan.

But now, his hand hanging in mid-air, he wasn't so sure.

A thought had come to him—one he should've considered earlier.

He kept inserting himself into her life.

At the masquerade when he'd claimed a dance...a month later, when he'd jumped into her carriage and spent the afternoon with her...even the idea for his noble deed at Hope House had sprung from her words.

And now, here he was, invading her evening meal.

But it had been a week, and he had this news to deliver —and he wanted to see her.

It was that brightness that sparked off the woman. She lived with such purpose and intention.

Purpose and intention.

He'd never known that interior spark—and having been a dedicated wastrel and rake didn't signify.

Except he knew why he kept inserting himself into her life.

Aye, there was Papa's ring that bound them.

But it was something else that had him here tonight, desperate for a glimpse of her.

He wanted some of her light for himself.

Right.

He released his hand and gave it permission to rap out three firm knocks.

His days as a rake had prepared him for entering through a side kitchen door. He'd done so under the cover of night on many an occasion. Generally, servants liked a rake.

Enlivened their gossip.

The door cracked a few inches open, and around solid oak peeked a house maid. He opened his mouth to deliver a greeting, but she craned her neck around to the room behind her and called out, "It's Lord Rhys Osborne."

A vertical line formed between his eyebrows. "You know who I am?"

The maid looked as if she were about to answer when a woman of greater size and authority took her place in the now fully open doorway. With her assured, direct gaze and the ring of keys hanging from her belt, it wasn't difficult to guess she was the housekeeper. "We're servants in a great household, Lord Rhys," said the formidable woman. "We know the names of all who enter."

That was him told.

The woman stood aside and allowed him entry into the kitchen aglow with candlelight and warmth from the ovens. At the far end of the long, low-ceilinged room sat the other servants gathered around a large rectangular table. As he'd suspected, they were taking their evening meal.

He scanned the heads for blonde curls—and found none.

"Now," said the housekeeper, "may we assist you in some way, Lord Rhys?" The woman was asking him very politely what in the blazes he was doing here.

He couldn't very well ask her to point him in the direction of Miss Birdwell. It would be indiscreet and possibly put her employment at risk.

So, he rummaged through his brain for a reason a reformed wastrel lord would intrude on the servants' evening meal and seized upon a thought so outlandish it might just be taken for the truth. "As it happens," he began, in very proper lord speak, "I'm in the process of establishing my own household. Upon my last visit, I was so impressed by the smooth running of Lord Percival's household, I thought I'd see how it was accomplished below stairs."

Life had taught him a little barefaced flattery never went amiss.

Except the incredulous lift of every brow in the room communicated he hadn't quite hit the mark.

The housekeeper nodded as if she were taking his words seriously and not trying to find his angle. "The first thing you'll do, Lord Rhys, is hire a well-disposed, trustworthy housekeeper, and she will fill out your household with well-disposed, trustworthy servants."

A smile stretched across his mouth, and he nodded, neither action deeply felt, but both expected in this extraordinary situation he'd put them all in. "Ah, yes, of course." Dimples flashing, he added a hasty, "Thank you."

His appreciation was met with a regal nod of the housekeeper's head. "My pleasure, Lord Rhys." She half turned and said over her shoulder, "Irwin?"

A tall lad of no more than seventeen years shuffled to his feet, his mouth still working on a bite of mutton.

"Please escort Lord Rhys to the drawing room." *Where he belongs*, she left unspoken. To Rhys, she continued, "You will find the family there, as they have finished taking their evening meal."

Rhys was left with no choice but to be escorted through the east wing of the Duke of Arundel's manse by the disgruntled Irwin, who couldn't hide his sulk at having been pulled away from his meal.

It felt like the longest walk in the history of walks. Like, when he arrived at his destination, he would be escorted to the naughty corner to have a long think about what had led him to this outcome.

What had he been thinking?

Being here…in Lord Percival's residence…*uninvited*.

He'd lost his bleeding mind.

That was what.

And here he'd thought his plan to grab a word with Miss Birdwell in the kitchen peerless.

He should have sent a note.

But now, intriguingly, he'd stumbled into a mystery— why wasn't Miss Birdwell taking her evening meal with the other servants, anyway?

Irwin entered the wide doorway of the drawing room and stood aside for Rhys to follow, whereupon the enormity of his mistake collapsed down on him. This wasn't the drawing room one invited acquaintances into. With its cozy, lived-in feel, this drawing room was for family and close friends. In other words, this drawing room wasn't for the likes of Lord Rhys Osborne.

"Lord Rhys Osborne," pronounced Irwin to the room at

large, then the servant spun on his heel and exited, presumably to return to the kitchen where he would promptly wolf down the remainder of his evening meal.

Though the room's occupants were scattered throughout—Bretagne seated in a worn leather wingback reading a newspaper...Lady Percival bent over an embroidery hoop...Miss Bretagne lounging on a sofa, flipping through the stack of correspondence on her lap...*Tilly*, who was seated at the back of the room behind a large table with several books spread open before her—the surprised lift of their four sets of eyebrows at his uninvited presence were identical.

As Lady Percival's mouth curved into a smile that would smooth over this no small bit of social awkwardness, Rhys noticed something else about this family drawing room.

Though Christmas Day was yet a fortnight away, some decorating had already begun on the mantle with a profusion of greenery—holly, ivy, and hawthorn—adorned with delicate gold bows and flanked by two large Christmas candles.

Unusual to decorate before Christmas Eve, but Rhys knew down to his bones it would've been all Miss Birdwell's doing.

The woman loved Christmas.

Until a few weeks ago, Rhys had never given a single thought to Christmas beyond the obligatory holiday meal with family, then the Boxing Day rounds to servants and tenants the following day. In truth, he'd always found the latter a chore. Well, wastrel rakes weren't known for putting others before themselves, were they?

His visit to Hope House had helped alter that view. The joy he'd brought the children with the toys and decorations. The joy he'd brought the women by being at their beck and call.

Tilly had been right to giggle.

It had been funny.

But it had been something else, too—*fun.*

Though run off his feet, he'd enjoyed himself.

But in the present situation he found himself in, it wasn't joy he'd brought, but consternation.

The scowl creasing Bretagne's forehead said as much.

The bewildered smile perched on Miss Bretagne's mouth said as much, too.

As for Miss Birdwell… She was watching him as one would an exotic animal that had escaped from the Tower of London.

"Lord Rhys," said Lady Percival in her soft Spanish accent, her striking green eyes encouraging, "what an unexpected delight. I'm afraid we're having a rather sedate night in, but won't you join us?"

Rhys found his feet moving, even as his mouth was having trouble. "I, *erm,* thought I would come and ask—"

Ask what?

He was saved from having to follow that sentence to its inevitable crashing conclusion, when Bretagne said, exasperation shimmering about him, "There have been no further developments about the ring." He added, "As I explained, I will contact you when that changes."

Miss Birdwell's head tipped, topaz-blue eyes subtly narrowed. "*Ring?*"

"I was helping Osborne recover a piece of his father's lost property," Bretagne said to the room.

Rhys couldn't help noticing Bretagne hadn't asked him to sit down.

Miss Birdwell's eyebrows reached for the ceiling. "Is that so, now?"

Bretagne's scowl returned. "Are you acquainted with one another?"

It was Miss Bretagne who answered. "Lord Rhys brought Christmas cheer to Hope House last week."

"Nobly motivated, I'm sure." If, at first, Bretagne had looked merely disinclined to make this easy on Rhys, he now looked plainly suspicious.

Rhys cleared his throat, deciding it best to return the subject to the safest topic. "I have a promising direction in regards to the ring."

Bretagne's air of expectancy increased, his near-black eyes asking, *Then why in the blazes have you barged into my house?*

Rhys supposed Bretagne's eyes had every right to ask that question—his mouth, too. He and Bretagne weren't actually friends, only friends of friends of friends, which didn't give Rhys the by-your-leave to pop by unannounced on any old evening.

With obvious reluctance, Bretagne folded his newspaper, set it aside, and unfurled his long, lean form. "Lord Rhys," he said, "have a cigar with me in the garden."

And so it transpired a few minutes later that Rhys was outside walking the grounds and smoking a cigar with Lord Percival Bretagne when his sole intention had been to see Miss Birdwell.

Lies, half-truths, and obscured intentions could get one into a right mess.

"So," said Bretagne on an exhalation of earthy cigar smoke, "if you aren't here about your father's ring, then *why* are you here?"

The directness of the question caught Rhys on the back foot. "Well, I—" It occurred to him that he was terribly unskilled at subterfuge.

He'd only ever been skilled at one thing, it seemed—being a rake.

Bretagne scrutinized him askance. "Are you attempting to court my daughter?"

Now, it was Rhys's brow's turn to lift with surprise.

Bretagne didn't wait for a response. "I'll say this once. Lucy is not for you."

Rhys couldn't even be offended. He knew his reputation. "I'm not here for that reason."

Bretagne caught his gaze and spent the next three seconds searching it. Finally, he nodded, apparently mollified by what he found there. "Then can you get on with explaining yourself?"

Rhys understood subtlety wouldn't suffice. "Miss Birdwell—"

Bretagne's straight dark eyebrows crashed together. "*Tilly?*"

"She takes meals with your family and spends evenings with you?"

Obviously, he hadn't come here to ask that question, but he found he wanted to know the answer.

"What of it?"

"Isn't she Lady Percival's servant?"

"I never took you for a snob, Osborne."

Rhys just kept getting it wrong, didn't he?

Bretagne snorted. "Tilly is my wife's servant as much as she could be anyone's servant."

Rhys didn't know how to reply to that, so he held his silence.

"Tilly is no one's servant," explained Bretagne. "She's family. Not in the literal sense, of course, but as good as."

"But she works as your wife's lady's maid."

"Because she wants to." Bretagne puffed his cigar. "Tilly doesn't have to do anything she doesn't want to. My wife has made that very clear to her."

"Yet she stays?"

"It's unorthodox," Bretagne allowed. "But my wife and Tilly have their own relationship."

Rhys heard the implication. Bretagne wouldn't be getting in the way of the bond his wife and Miss Birdwell shared.

"An interesting *on dit* hit my ears a couple of weeks ago, which I'd ignored," continued Bretagne.

"Quite a few *on dit*s must cross your path." It was why he'd come to Bretagne with the problem of Papa's missing signet ring in the first place.

"This one concerned *you.*"

"Well, I *have* made something of a spectacle of myself in the past."

He was buying time and knew it.

"*Recent,*" said Bretagne. A quirk at the corner of his mouth indicated he might've started enjoying himself.

"Oh?"

"You were observed at Mivart's with a rather eye-catching blonde."

Rhys remained silent. Nothing was to be gained by lying to Lord Percival Bretagne.

"So, I'll ask you this once. Why were you gadding about Town with my wife's lady's maid?"

A sudden, inexplicable, and utterly unexpected urge to defend roared up inside Rhys. "Her name is Miss Birdwell."

"I know her name," said Bretagne, plainly irked. "My question is—why do you?"

"It's a long story."

"I have time."

Rhys found he wasn't inclined to bend or stand down beneath Bretagne's pressure. "A story that's between her and me."

That got a lift of Bretagne's eyebrows, and Rhys couldn't help feeling a moment's satisfaction. Under no circumstances would he betray Miss Birdwell and tell Bretagne the story of how they'd become entangled with each other, which had involved her swiping an invitation not intended for her and sneaking out to a masquerade ball where she'd danced, cheated a card cheat, won Papa's ring for herself, and generally had one of the best nights of her life.

Rhys could neither begrudge her that night nor reveal it to another living soul.

Once Bretagne comprehended he wouldn't be getting any information on that subject from Rhys, he said, "You're here for Tilly, yes?"

It wasn't a question.

It was a demand.

"Yes."

"And why is that?"

"She's helping me."

Which was both true and untrue, at once.

She was both helping him recover Papa's ring and obstructing him at the same time.

But *more* was true, too.

She was helping him in ways he didn't understand, but felt.

Bretagne's eyes narrowed into near-black daggers poised to wound at the slightest misstep from Rhys. "You're not toying with her?"

"No."

"You won't hurt her?"

"*Never.*"

He'd nearly growled the word.

In his entire life, he'd never spoken a word with as much intensity.

Bretagne stubbed out his cigar in a dish outside the French doors. Before he reentered the drawing room, he caught Rhys's gaze. "Then I'll leave you to it."

With that, Bretagne left Rhys outside to reckon with those words, alone and, frankly, unbalanced.

To his ears they sounded suspiciously like permission.

Permission to court Miss Birdwell.

Which, in his nine and twenty years, was a first.

9

From her place behind the table, Tilly held an unimpeded view of the doors the men had disappeared through.

The room had gone quiet without them in it. Lucy continued flipping through her correspondence. Isabel remained concentrated on her embroidery, but with a newly heightened air of watchfulness about her. And Tilly kept her gaze cast down toward the books spread before her.

But her stillness was a façade.

Inside, she was stirred.

Lord Rhys...here.

When, after an interminable number of seconds and minutes, he walked into the room through the doors he'd disappeared through looking like he'd stumbled out the other side of a hurricane, she understood he'd braved that hurricane for one reason.

Her.

While she didn't know what to think about that, her body seemed to have an idea about how to feel about it.

She'd always liked champagne, and now she knew exactly how a champagne coupe felt with all those sparkling, little bubbles fizzing inside it.

A new feeling, this one.

His silver eyes found hers, and like that, she was too full of this feeling to draw or release another breath.

"A letter from Mina!" exclaimed Lucy, bolting upright as she cracked the seal.

Tilly only realized Lord Rhys had been moving toward her when he stopped and asked, "Mina?"

"Miss Mina Radclyffe," Isabel explained.

"She's my step-sister," said Lucy, distractedly, for her eyes were already scanning the contents of the letter. "And best bosom friend."

Lord Rhys returned his attention to Tilly. "And you, Miss Birdwell, do you know Miss Radclyffe?"

Tilly nodded. "I met her two or three times before she sailed off to Japan a few years back."

"*Japan?*"

"She has Japanese ancestry," cut in Isabel.

"A right beauty she is," said Tilly.

"But that mind of hers might even surpass it," said Lord Percival, not bothering to look up from the newspaper he'd resumed reading.

Lord Rhys lifted his brow as if to say, *Well*, and Tilly felt the urge to giggle, which she suppressed with a smile.

"All right." Lucy lowered the letter to her lap and addressed the room. "She is returning next year." Her mouth was racing as quickly as her mind with excitement. "Which means I can start readying the house on Queen Street for her arrival."

Lord Percival lowered his newspaper. "Is that still the plan, then?" One couldn't take his tone for pleased.

"Of course, it is, Father," said Lucy, all breezy indifference.

"You'll have a butler," he said, firm. "Of my choosing."

"But we'll have Mrs. Bloomquist as our housekeeper," countered Lucy.

No mistaking that stubborn set to Lord Percival's jaw. "Does she know how to handle weaponry?"

A moment ticked past while Lucy gave the question her full consideration. "Honestly? Likely."

Tilly agreed.

She'd only met Mrs. Bloomquist on the rare occasion, but the woman was formidable. After all, she'd been the headmistress of The Progressive School for Young Ladies and the Education of Their Minds, which had been founded by Lucy's mother, Lady St. Alban. Tilly felt certain Mrs. Bloomquist could handle herself in any situation that presented itself.

"All right, Father," said an exasperated Lucy. "We'll have a butler, too."

"And the man will be of my—"

"Of your choosing." She exhaled an irritated huff through her nose. "But Mrs. Bloomquist won't like it."

"What is the purpose of Queen Street?" asked Lord Rhys, addressing Lucy.

"It's to be our ladies' den."

"Your *ladies' den?*" He looked both perplexed and intrigued.

Tilly almost snorted.

A rake would be, wouldn't he?

"Oh, yes," said Lucy.

"That's an unusual arrangement for unmarried ladies," he said diplomatically.

"Which is why they shall have a butler with military experience," said Lord Percival without looking up from his newspaper.

Lucy rolled her eyes, but let her pa's words stand. "Tell me, Lord Rhys," she began, and Tilly recognized that note of mischief in her voice, "do you have your own flat of rooms?"

"I do."

Lucy spread her hands wide. "And there's nothing unusual in that."

"There isn't," he said, slowly. He clearly knew full well he was being led into a trap.

That little smile sparkling in Lucy's eyes said she had him. "Then why can't we ladies enjoy that same freedom?"

Lord Rhys smiled a smile that must've melted many a dress off many a lady. "Why, indeed?"

"Oh!" Lucy shot to her feet. "I must tell Cousin Hugh. He will want to know. I think. Actually, I'm not sure how he will feel about it. He's been so involved with Lady Rosalind."

"Are they yet engaged?" asked Isabel without looking up from her embroidery hoop.

"Nothing in the gossip rags yet," said Lucy, slowly. "But

when the heir of a future duke courts the daughter of a current duke...*hmm*." Her feet were on the move. "Well, seeing as he's just in the other wing of the house, I'll pop by his rooms. Who doesn't enjoy receiving news of old friends?"

And with that, Lucy was gone.

Leaving a little awkward silence in her absence.

Lord Percival snorted and said, "Daughters," shaking his head at his newspaper.

With a smile curving her mouth that said, *Daughters, indeed*, Isabel pulled another stitch through her embroidery piece.

Tilly's gaze had returned, unseeing, to the books laid out before her.

And Lord Rhys's gaze remained where it had been most of this time—on her.

"What do you have there, Miss Birdwell?" he asked, his feet following each word, step by step leading him closer.

Tilly must look up and answer.

She understood that.

But for the first time in her entire life, she felt...*shy*.

It had to do with this lord coming here uninvited to spend time with, of all people, *her*.

Only when he'd stopped at the other side of the table, leaving her no option, her gaze lifted and met his, aye, *shyly*. "I like to study," she said, an unaccountable defensiveness creeping into her tone.

His brow lifted. "You're a student of the"—he cocked his head at a ninety-degree angle to be able to read the upside-down books—"*Classics?*"

It took her a tick of time to parse his meaning. "Oh, you mean because these drawings and paintings are Greek and Roman." She remembered that period was called Classical. "I'm studying their clothes."

His mouth turned down at the corners. "Interesting pastime."

"It's not a pastime." There was that defensiveness again. "What you see here in these illustrations of statues is the history of fashion."

He appeared to give her words consideration. "I never thought of it like that."

"After my friend Nell taught me how to read a few years back," she continued, "I took to books. They look dead boring from the outside, but it amazes the mind what they hold inside."

She couldn't help noticing how he was looking at her as she spoke.

How he always looked at her as she spoke.

Like he was interested, genuinely.

Another wash of champagne bubbles glittered through her.

Across the room, Isabel set her embroidery hoop down and stretched her arms over her head with a loud yawn. "I think it's early to bed for me," she said. "How about you, husband?"

"I have another article to—"

Isabel cleared her throat. "You look tired, Percy."

Lord Percival met his wife's gaze for a full three seconds. "Right." He folded the newspaper and came to his feet. "Good night, Tilly. Osborne, you know the way out."

And with that, Isabel left the room with her husband—leaving Tilly alone with Lord Rhys.

The air felt different now that it was just him and her.

Though, why should it?

Except, simply, when a woman was alone in a room with Lord Rhys Osborne she noticed.

"I have a question I would like to ask you, Miss Birdwell."

"You invited yourself here tonight to ask me a question?"

The smile he gave her brought out his dimples. "It wasn't smoothly done of me, was it?"

"Can't say it was."

"I came here thinking I'd catch you in the kitchen at the evening meal."

"Ah."

"And to inform you of the date and location for my second noble deed."

"You could've sent a note."

"I could've."

But he hadn't.

That was what was left unsaid.

He'd wanted to come here.

He'd wanted to see her.

Lawks.

She might be in trouble.

How was a woman to withstand the charms of the reformed-perhaps-unreformed rake Lord Rhys Osborne?

"But then I wouldn't be able to ask you a question that's

been on my mind since we spoke at Hope House." He hesitated. "In the scullery."

In the scullery, they'd spoken of her past.

And now he had a question?

She mustered up some bravado and opened her mouth. "What's your question?"

He shifted on his feet, looking a hair anxious, and it only increased his attractiveness. "You don't have to answer if you don't want to."

"All right." Now she really wanted to hear this question of his.

"What's your dream, Miss Birdwell?" He looked as earnest as she'd ever seen him. "You mentioned having one, and I must confess to finding myself incredibly intrigued."

Her? A woman who *incredibly intrigued* Lord Rhys Osborne?

Blow her down.

Perhaps it was his earnestness or perhaps it was being the object of his intrigue, but she found herself saying, "I told you what my dream once was."

He nodded.

"But that's the sort of dream little girls have, innit? So, when Isabel came along and swept me into her world, that was when my life really began, and I became skilled at something that makes me proud." She swallowed against a sudden knot in her throat. "I never thought I could be proud of myself."

The way he was watching her made her feel like she could tell him anything.

So maybe that was why she was.

"Isabel and her sister, Eva, have this dressmaking business together, and it got me to thinking and dreaming. Not about making dresses, but a business where I can instruct folk how to make themselves fashionable. You see, being a stylish lady ain't just about wearing a pretty French dress or the most expensive strand of South Sea pearls. It's how a lady wears that dress and them pearls, and the thing I've learned is that most women—ladies and otherwise—they're not born knowing how to accomplish that. But me? I was." She shrugged. "And there is my business opportunity."

A few beats of time ticked past where Lord Rhys studied her silently and she sat very still with her hands clasped in her lap, fingernails digging half-moons into her palms.

"When do you plan to start your business?" he asked, at last.

She didn't hesitate. This was a point of pride for her. "In fifteen years."

His brow wrinkled. *"Fifteen years?"* He looked genuinely perplexed. "How old are you? Twenty…"

"I'm five-and-twenty years old," she stated, sounding no small bit huffy.

"So, when you start your business, you'll be—"

"Forty years old."

He was proper scowling at her now. "That's too far in the future."

"Well, that game of Loo brought it in by a few years, didn't it?"

His brow released as if an unanticipated thought had struck him. "Is this about money?"

"Aren't most things?" The good and the bad, she wouldn't say, but truly, lords and their loose association with the concept of economics.

"Why don't you ask Lady Percival to help you?"

"I'll not be repaying the new life she gave me by begging from her. My business will start as I mean it to go on—under my own steam. I'll not borrow a penny to see it through."

A few seconds ticked past while he churned her words, and her blood cooled a few degrees. "And those books," he said, pointing, "are of use to you in your endeavor?"

"Aye, they are," she said, nodding, relieved the conversation had taken a different angle. "The thing about fashion and style is, when you know the past, you can see the future."

Surprise shone in his eyes. "Is that so?"

"What's in the past always comes around again is what I've found in all the books I've read. But in a way that feels new."

"Would you mind showing me your favorite?"

Tilly understood his question wasn't one simple question.

It was a question that didn't only have an answer.

It was a question that led to consequences.

"All right," she said, unable to say anything else.

The thing was, she might have a curiosity regarding those consequences.

It was no wonder Lord Rhys had been a rake.

Seducing would've been as easy as breathing for him.

Like she'd known he would do, he came around to her side of the table.

Consequence number one.

She flipped pages until she found her favorite illustration, and he bent over her shoulder to inspect it.

Consequence number two.

On her next inhalation, she filled her lungs with air and his scent of amber and citrus.

Consequence number three.

Oh, those consequences just kept adding up, didn't they?

They fueled a feeling inside her—a wild, effervescent feeling…a reckless feeling.

"What is it you like about this one?" he asked, his voice low and velvet, closer than she'd expected.

A few further consequences presented themselves—consequences that led down paths one couldn't turn back from.

On a deep breath, she settled back, putting precious inches between herself and the mouth that had asked the question.

Lord Rhys blinked.

It occurred to Tilly no woman had ever deviated from the path he led her down.

Something opaque registered behind his eyes, and he straightened before cocking his hip against the table, putting even more inches between her and his mouth.

She should feel better, steadier in her intentions.

She wasn't sure she did.

For certain parts of her had begun to wonder what his mouth would feel like.

Certain parts of her wondered about his intentions.

But more, certain parts wondered about her own intentions.

She gave herself a good shake of the mind and forced herself to return to his question.

Something about her favorite…

Right.

She cleared her throat and pressed a finger to the illustration of the statue of Venus that was discovered on the Greek island of Milos several years ago.

Lord Rhys lifted an eyebrow, a smile tickling about his mouth. "She isn't wearing much."

"But it isn't about what she is wearing, don't you see?"

He squinted. "Hmm."

"It's about how every element hangs together," she continued, fervent, determined he would, indeed, see. "She *is* nude on her upper half, but look at the way her hair is pulled back into a bun, neat as a pin. If all that hair was hanging loose with her bosom to the breeze like that, she would look a right hoyden, wouldn't she?"

He nodded, slowly, as if understanding were, at last, sinking in.

"But the way everything fits together, no one could take her for anything but a goddess. Just look at all that power coming off her." Tilly tapped her finger. "And that's style."

"Ah." He reached out and flipped through the pages of a different book. "What about this one?"

It took her a moment to register the image he was

pointing out, for her gaze had fixed on his large hand…his long, masculine fingers.

She cleared her throat in an attempt to corral her attention. "That one has a direct line to the fashion of twenty years ago. See the band below her bosom there?"

"Aye."

"That was the Empire silhouette of dresses around the turn of the century, and here is a Greek statue wearing that same style three thousand years ago."

There was no other way of putting it, Lord Rhys looked impressed. "You are a scholar, Miss Birdwell."

A scholar… Blow her down.

Miss Tilly Birdwell, a scholar.

"You see," she continued, his praise spurring her on, "the dress is itself, but *how* it's worn is style. Take this one." She pointed to an illustration in a different book. "See how the fabric drapes diagonally across the statue's chest here?"

"Mm-hmm."

"It leads the eye up to her neck when the hair is pulled back, revealing that elegant line there."

"Ah."

"And this line here?" She traced her finger along the curve of the statue's neck.

"Yeah?"

"The right hairstyle can make *it* the point of focus, if a lady wants it to be."

"This line here?" came the velvet question.

So caught up in educating Lord Rhys, she only realized how close he'd drawn when she felt the touch—a long, masculine finger tracing the exposed column of her throat.

Every sense in her body snapped to life.

Heightened, that was how she felt…*aware.*

Breathless and full to brimming with those champagne bubbles, she found herself swaying into that light touch of his finger leaving alive, little sparks in its wake.

Which consequence were they on now? *Number four?… Five?*

"Or with a curl positioned just so at the collarbone." Her finger continued its progress. "The décolletage would be the focal point."

In the way her finger progressed on the page, his progressed on her body, tracing along her collarbone to indent at the base of her throat—hesitating there.

This wasn't mere breathlessness.

This was what it was to be in thrall to a man.

And it would be *this* man.

"Or," she said, no longer able to recognize her own voice, such a raw-edged scrape it had become against her throat, "the lightest touch of rouge on the bottom lip."

Until this very moment, she'd never fully compre-hended the power of words.

That they could make the entire world stop spinning and go completely still.

From the corner of her eye, she detected it—*movement* —and his fingers were beneath her chin, light, but insis-tent, guiding her to face him, her head tipping back, her eyes meeting his.

She'd only met Lord Rhys Osborne, reformed rake.

But here, holding her gaze with intensity and intent, was that other Lord Rhys—the *un*reformed rake.

"A touch of rouge *here*?" asked this unreformed rake.

To illustrate his question, he pressed his thumb to her bottom lip, the calloused pad rough as it skated deliberately across that sensitive skin.

Her gaze locked onto his, she nodded.

Another of those world-gone-still moments passed, the intent within his silver-gray eyes unwavering, as he angled down and replaced his thumb with his mouth. He sucked her bottom lip into his mouth, his tongue gliding across, languid and expert. Oh, but weren't his beautiful lips as soft and firm, capable and skilled, as she'd thought they would be?

A spell wove around and through her.

That was how she would explain it to herself later.

A spell.

His large hand slid to the back of her head, steadying her, as he pressed forward, deepening the kiss, his mouth firmer, more insistent, as he touched his tongue to hers. She inhaled a gasp. It wasn't that she didn't know what to do, but never had she taken such pleasure from it. She reached up, touching trembly fingertips to his cheek...his jaw...around to the hair that curled up at the nape of his neck, those hairs soft and ticklish, as she swayed forward, her tongue tangling with his.

He groaned into her mouth, that deep, masculine utterance resonating through her, becoming one with her in all its longing and ache.

Her body understood that soul-deep groan and echoed it.

It resonated not only through her, it resonated *with* her.

"Oh, Miss Birdwell," he muttered against her lips. "You're so sweet."

Sweet.

In her life, she'd been referred to by a multitude of words—*saucy...mouthy...bold...bawd...* Worse words than those, too.

But not *sweet.*

Yet this man looked at her—*saw* her—in a way she'd never been looked at or seen.

To him, she was sweet.

"Lord Rhys," she whispered, knowing what she must do.

He angled back, just enough to meet her eyes...just enough to break the kiss. Panting and out of breath, they stared out at each other, both knowing the kiss had needed to end.

It could go no further.

Ironic, that, considering both their pasts.

But in her past, she'd never felt *this*—that she wanted more...that she might perish in her lonely bed tonight without it.

He angled away far enough so he could stand.

And as she'd remained sitting, her eyeline happened to be on a level with his waist and...the cockstand raging beneath his trousers.

Lawks.

It didn't take a stretch of the imagination to understand what a fine specimen of a cockstand it was, either.

The sort of cockstand to take a gel's breath away—and have her aching thighs squeezing together.

How could something that wasn't new to her—*kisses... raging cockstands*—feel so new?

How was it she could want something so desperately that she'd never truly wanted all those years ago?

And the answer—undeniable, simple, and true—came to her.

Choice.

He might've started this kiss, but she'd chosen it.

It was the first time she'd ever chosen a kiss outside the parameters of a transaction—of her own free will.

And it felt good.

It felt free, in every sense of the word.

A throat cleared, and her gaze startled up.

She'd been caught staring at his fine specimen of a cockstand.

A smile perched upon his lips, his eyes asked, *Got your fill?*

And she suspected her eyes of responding with something like, *Not hardly.*

"Miss Birdwell—"

"Tilly."

"*Tilly*, will you meet me on the corner of Piccadilly and St. James's Street at eleven o'clock tomorrow night to witness my second noble deed?"

She gave a light clearing of her throat. "Aye."

How shy her voice had gone.

"Until then..." He bent down and caught her mouth with his one last time.

And when he broke away and strode from the room,

Tilly remained precisely as he'd left her—sitting forward in her chair...mouth waiting for his return.

She touched trembly fingertips to kiss-crushed lips.

This desire she'd experienced—the remnants that yet fizzed through her—it wasn't just that it was new to her.

She'd never known it existed.

Not for women, anyway.

Desire, it had always seemed to her, was the exclusive privilege of men.

But here she was in this room, alone with a different knowledge.

And she knew something else, too.

That spell Lord Rhys Osborne—*Rhys*—had woven around and through her...

It yet held fast.

10

―――

NEXT NIGHT

His feet a quick clip along Bennet Street, the collar of his greatcoat flipped to guard against a north wind holding more than a hint of northern chill, Rhys pulled his silver watch from his pocket.

10 o'clock.

He had exactly one hour until he was to meet Tilly on the corner of Piccadilly and St. James's Street—and much to accomplish between now and then.

And though he should've been concentrating on the task before him, it was Tilly who claimed the entirety of his thoughts.

Oh, the woman was on his mind.

Well, her and their kiss.

The kiss…

He hadn't been able not to touch her.

Then he hadn't been able not to kiss her.

That was the thing—and it plagued his mind.

Those were excuses his old self would've made.

133

Tilly was temptation personified, and he'd never found much success in resisting that which tempted him.

Which was why this last year, he'd removed himself entirely from temptation's path.

That, more than anything, was the secret of his reformation—to hold himself so far away from temptation that he couldn't immediately act on any urge that entered his mind or pulsed through his body.

He hadn't planned for Tilly, though.

Yet, as a temptation, she was different, too.

He was having difficulty explaining it to himself, even, for the woman was so incredibly desirable in all the purely superficial ways one could ask for—of face and figure…the sparkle in her eyes…her vivacity…the breezy trill of her giggle.

Oh, yes, she was a knocker of a woman, but she possessed other qualities that drew him in.

Qualities his unreformed self had given not one toss about.

Tilly had brains and goals…ambitions and dreams…the determination to see them through.

Tilly, in her fully revealed self, was irresistible.

There.

There was the difference between who he was now and the man he once was.

His former self wouldn't consider Tilly fully revealed to him yet, for he hadn't tupped her.

Perhaps he had grown beyond that person, the wastrel rake.

Which wasn't to say he didn't want to tup her.

But he didn't *only* want to tup her, which he supposed was growth.

He rounded the corner from Bennet Street and onto St. James's. White's stood a block ahead across the street. It was there that Rhys would attempt to set in motion tonight's second noble deed.

It was strange, but his way of thinking about Papa's signet ring had shifted. While he was as determined as he'd ever been to return the ring to where it belonged, the urgency had diminished—for one reason alone.

The ring was in Tilly's trustworthy hands.

Truly, the woman might've become an obsession.

He took the short set of stairs up to White's front door two at a time, both a spring to his step and a tetchy energy shimmering through him. A year, it had been, since he'd walked through this door.

The doorman nodded as he stood aside, recognizing Rhys on sight. "Lord Rhys, it is a pleasure to see you."

Rhys gave a nod and smile of greeting as he stepped into the entrance hall, where he declined to hand over his hat and coat to a footman. He shouldn't be here long, if all went to plan.

He made an immediate left into the morning room with its famous bow window that overlooked St. James's Street. This was where the dandies liked to congregate during the day to watch and comment on the promenade of other dandies on the sidewalk. Of course, at a quarter past ten in the evening, the dandies all had to make do with each other inside the club, as the street outside had gone dark.

Copious amounts of wine, whisky, brandy, and port helped them make do with circumstances.

Rhys scanned the room for his quarry—and encountered no luck.

He would have to venture deeper into the club.

His bad luck continued when a voice rang out, "Lord Rhys!"

A dozen soused smiles turned his way and eager hands waved him inside the room.

He'd known this would happen. That he would be invited for a night's carousing.

And he'd known he would have to resist.

With a smile of apology, he spread his hands wide and backed away. "Apologies, gentlemen, but I have business to attend this evening."

"*Business?*" came a shout, followed by an immediate roar of laughter. "What's that?"

But it was all at Rhys's back, for he was on the move, heading straight for the billiard room. Maybe he would encounter some luck in finding the man he sought there.

His string of rotten luck persisted, however, for instead of the man he sought, he found an altogether different man bent over his billiards cue—a man Rhys was most definitely *not* seeking.

His hope that he hadn't been spotted was dashed when a firm, "Rhys!" met his retreating back. He stopped dead in his tracks, closed his eyes for a second and groaned.

He had no choice but to double back.

The man had straightened to his familiar height of six feet plus a few inches—precisely the same height as Rhys, in fact—and was regarding Rhys with the lift of a single black eyebrow.

"Brother," said Rhys in greeting to his older brother, Lord Jasper Osborne.

Not the heir, but the spare.

Jasper handed his cue to a waiting footman and came around the table. His brother didn't speak again until he'd stopped a few feet away and given Rhys a thorough up-and-down. "Papa has this strange notion about you."

Jasper wasn't known for his small talk.

"Oh?"

"That you've left off being a waster."

Even as he experienced a sliver of annoyance at that glint of doubt in his brother's eyes, something warmed inside Rhys.

Papa actually believed that of him?

Which was why he said more boldly than he felt, "I have."

Jasper's head cocked to the side. "Then what are you doing *here*?"

"It's a long story."

Jasper looked disinclined to relent. "I have time."

He was calling Rhys's bluff.

Brothers could do that with one another.

Except Rhys wasn't bluffing—and he didn't have time.

In less than an hour, Tilly would be on that street corner—waiting for him.

"Some other time," he said, his feet itching to be on the move.

His brother, of course, wouldn't believe him.

Well, if he were Jasper, he wouldn't believe him, either.

In his nine-and-twenty years, Rhys had done little-to-nothing to inspire belief.

But that was changing.

"You'll want to avoid the dining room," said Jasper, holding out a hand for the footman to return his billiards cue to him.

"Oh?"

"Benedict is there."

Benedict.

Their eldest brother—*the heir*—who hadn't had a smile for Rhys in, at least, fifteen years.

Rhys nodded his thanks and pivoted on his heel.

Best he avoided the dining room.

As he made his way up the staircase to the first floor, he decided there would be no more distractions. He reached the landing, turned a sharp right, and headed directly for the room where he knew deep in his gut he would find the man he sought—the gaming room.

At the wide doorway, a slick of perspiration coated his palms. Every cell in his body both demanded he turn around and abandon his plan *and* demanded he enter and assume his rightful place at the tables—and give in to what was only natural.

So, it was the sharp edge of a razor blade he navigated as he stepped into the room and became both part of its lively milieu and apart from it at once.

The man he sought sat at neither the Faro nor the Whist tables. But then, Rhys hadn't expected him there.

Deeper into the room he moved until, at last, Rhys spotted him standing at a Hazard table.

Whitty.

Rhys had first met the Right Honorable Viscount Bartram Whitmore at Eton College, where they'd both been sent to board at the ripe old age of thirteen. As Whitty had been a viscount before he could walk, he'd been assured of his place in the hierarchy of the world and what his title and wealth bought him, which was *everything*.

It had even bought him more than a few friends.

But not Rhys.

From the start, their kinship had been fundamentally rooted in an aligned goal—to have fun at any and all costs.

And how they'd succeeded.

With Whitty's wealth and recklessness, and Rhys's looks and charm, they'd cut a wide swath through, first, school—where admittedly the stakes had been low—then on through society where the stakes seemed to rise higher each passing year.

Whitty even had a pet phrase: *Can't be arsed a whit.*

Whitty thought it the wittiest cant ever coined, and Rhys hadn't reckoned it was his place to disabuse his friend of the notion, even as Whitty said—or shouted, depending on his state of inebriation—the phrase on at least a dozen occasions on any given night, particularly after midnight.

So, here was Rhys in White's intending to speak to his oldest friend—his oldest comrade in dissolution.

"Can't be arsed a whit!" cut through the din.

Rhys's feet gathered pace as he edged through the crowd, dodging and returning greetings as he went. In the general sense, Lord Rhys Osborne was liked by all—with the exception of a few husbands.

At last, he reached the Hazard table and took quick measure of Whitty. It had been several months since he'd last laid eyes on his old friend. That intervening time hadn't been kind to Whitty, who'd gained a good stone about the middle and dark circles beneath his eyes. In truth, he looked closer to fifty than thirty.

Which gave Rhys a measure of confidence in what he was about to attempt.

It wouldn't only be noble deed number two.

He would be helping Whitty, and wasn't that what friends did for each other?

Whitty's enlivened gaze lifted from the green baize of the Hazard table. As he registered Rhys's approach, a broad smile broke across his sweat-sheened face. "As I live and breathe, if it ain't Lord Rhys Osborne," he exclaimed in that jolly way of his.

Rhys returned his smile, genuinely glad to see his old friend. "Whitty."

"Come over here, old chap." Whitty clapped Rhys on the back once he'd crowded next to him at the table. "Now," he said, holding out his open palm whereupon perched two dice, "blow on my dice. I've been on a bad run."

Rhys snorted and blew on Whitty's dice, which he then tossed and immediately threw out.

His friend groaned, and Rhys said, "You know I've never had luck with the dice."

Which was true.

Though he'd only realized how unlucky after this last year—after he'd stopped.

Whitty waved Rhys's words away. "Can't be arsed a whit."

It surely wasn't the second time he'd uttered those words tonight—nor the last.

Whitty used the back of his hand to swipe a bead of sweat off his forehead. "What are you doing here, anyway? Haven't seen you in—" His eyes screwed up toward the ceiling. "When was the last time I laid eyes on you, anyway?"

"Thought I'd check in on an old friend," Rhys replied neutrally.

Whitty cast his gaze around the room. "Who's that?"

"*You*, Whitty."

No one would mistake Whitty for the sharpest knife in the block, but somehow that was part of his charm.

Whitty gave him a jovial slap on the back. "Jolly grand to see you, old chap. So, are we to have a night?"

"We are," said Rhys.

Though not in the way Whitty would be expecting.

Better that was left to discover later, rather than reveal now.

"You know, Ossie," began Whitty, as if he were concentrated in thought, "there's something in the air. I have a feeling your Hazard luck is due for a turnaround."

Rhys found a set of dice in his hand and a dozen pairs of expectant eyes on him.

"I'll stake you." Whitty slid his stack of markers in front of Rhys. "You just roll, old man."

The slick of sweat that had coated his palms now pinpricked across Rhys's entire body. He had a choice—place the dice down and walk away or…toss them.

If he walked away, though, he would be leaving Whitty and abandoning his plan for the night—and his second noble deed.

And, really, what was one throw of the dice, anyway?

It was true, what he'd said to Whitty. He had no luck with dice.

So, wouldn't it be better to roll and throw out?

One and done.

Then he could move into the next stage of this night—and its true purpose.

His hand began moving, the dice rattling in his palm, their weight so familiar, his heart a hammer in his chest, the blood thundering through his veins… roaring in his ears, so he could hear nothing but the voice urging him to give over. He'd suspected it was there all this time, lying in wait—and now he had it confirmed.

This voice…this urge…would never disappear.

It was part of him, as sure as the cells that composed his physical being.

As the dice flew from his hand and he called out, "Seven," how good…how *right*…it felt to give over. The dice rolled and tumbled to a stop and what should they show but a two and a five…

Seven.

"See?" proclaimed Whitty. "You've been shoring up luck all these months. Now, do it again."

Again, Rhys was holding dice, feeling their weight in his hand before letting them fly.

And again, he nicked the main and he was off on the best run of his life.

Everyone crowding around the table knew it...the blood screaming hot through his veins knew it, too.

Oh, it felt good.

And *right*.

Like he was back where he belonged.

He could stay here all night—even forever.

Forever.

The idea of that forever—forever at the tables...forever in the welcoming bosom of vice—snapped something awake inside him.

That forever suddenly felt like a prison sentence.

He dug his watch from his pocket.

Five minutes to eleven.

Five minutes from now, Tilly would be standing on the corner of Piccadilly and St. James's, waiting for him.

Trusting him to be there.

And one thing he understood with more clarity than he'd felt since entering White's tonight was he would never break Tilly's trust.

Not even for another winning roll of the dice.

Again, he felt the dice in his hand.

This time, he set them on green baize without rolling.

This was a first.

Not once in his life had he ever left a table when he was on a winning streak.

The crowd gathered round the table groaned, but this

determination inside him had turned into hard-tempered steel.

"What is this?" exclaimed Whitty, looking confused and betrayed.

"Come with me," said Rhys. He knew that wild, reckless glint in his friend's eyes. His blood was het up with the need for more action tonight.

"On to Brooks's, then?" Whitty began nodding, as if he'd answered his own question. "Excellent idea. Got to spread the luck."

"Actually," said Rhys, "I have another idea."

Whitty's eyes went even brighter. "Oh?"

Doubt pinged through Rhys. When he'd devised this plan for his second noble deed, perhaps he'd focused on the idealized version rather than the realities, for Whitty was practically panting with excitement, like his best bosom friend was about to present him with a night that was truly novel, possibly the best night of his life.

That was the gambler's dream, wasn't it?

Always chasing the best luck.

Always chasing the best night of their life.

Always chasing, never looking back and realizing their best, most lucky night had been the first night all those years and nights ago.

But perhaps this night would be the luckiest, just not in the way Whitty expected.

Perhaps his friend would look back on *this* night as the one that finally got his life moving in a meaningful direction.

Perhaps.

"Follow me." Rhys's feet were already on the move.

He didn't look back.

He now had three minutes to be on that street corner, and as much as he wanted to have done with his second noble deed, Tilly was the bigger priority.

If Whitty followed, he followed.

If he didn't, he didn't.

When had the priorities in Rhys's life so rearranged themselves that Tilly was now at the top?

11

Her feet planted on the corner of Piccadilly and St. James's Street, Tilly shifted from foot to foot, staving off the chill that wanted to creep in between the woolen layers of her clothes, and wondered what in the blazes had possessed her to agree to this.

A noble deed in *this* part of town where all the aristocratic midnight carousing happened?

As if the universe sought to illustrate her question, a gaggle of drunken, overloud lordlings staggered so close she had to step out of their way or be plowed over.

And even as she doubted her blooming mind for having agreed, she knew why she had.

Because it was Rhys who had asked.

She was right to doubt her mind.

Except it wasn't only her mind making these decisions, but other parts of her, too—her fingers to touch him…her lips to kiss him…

And there was this other place, too.

A place in the center of her chest that by turns contracted and expanded and *ached*.

So much of her had been involved in the decision that had her standing on this street corner.

All of it sparked by that kiss last night.

Lawks.

The champagne bubbles still fizzed through her blood.

Others had noticed, too.

At the breakfast table this morning, Lucy had taken one look at her, then proceeded to giggle through the entire meal. Lord Percival had shot Tilly the lift of a single eyebrow. Isabel had been quiet in that respectful way of hers. And when Tilly said she was going out tonight on an errand—no more sneaking out for her— instead of asking what sort of errand she was embarking upon at night, Isabel had simply replied, "Tilly, be careful."

Tilly knew what they all thought.

That she was carrying on with a wastrel rake.

And she supposed she was.

Except, her heart didn't believe what the mind should on that front.

She believed Rhys.

He no longer wanted to be that wastrel rake.

He was trying.

And she felt a deep kinship with that sort of striving.

That striving to be better.

To better oneself.

Ahead, a pair of wasters managed to sort of cascade down the front steps of White's without falling. She began to turn away and froze. One of those carousers—the tall one—had a very, very familiar way about him.

She squinted through the dim light.

In fact…that taller carouser wasn't only familiar, he was none other than Lord Rhys Osborne shuffling up the street.

The flare of outrage that blazed through her was instantaneous.

The cheek!

Once he and the other rotter with him came within shouting distance, she let fly. "You've got some brass, Rhys Osborne, inviting me here to…to…*what*? Bear witness to your carousing? Noble deed, my arse!"

"Tilly, Tilly, Tilly," he said—*pleaded*. "It's not what it looks like."

Mouth clamped shut, she exhaled through her nose and crossed her arms over her chest and waited, her foot tapping the cobblestones.

He waved a hand toward the fellow beside him. "I would like to introduce you to the Right Honorable Viscount Whitmore."

Rhys didn't sound drunk as a piper, she would give him that.

The lord beside him—*Viscount Whitmore*—gave a wobbly bow that listed to the left. "A lady such as thy lovely self can call me Whitty." He rubbed his nose with the back of his hand. "Everyone does, anyway."

Tilly saw a few things at once.

It was this lord who was three sheets to the wind, not Rhys.

And she liked this Whitty.

Oh, he possessed the look of an absolute waster, but he had kind eyes.

Her umbrage fell away. She still didn't know what this night was about, but she was intrigued. "And you can call me Tilly." She added on a laugh, "Everyone does."

Rhys searched her eyes for the split of a second, long enough for her to know what he was looking for. She offered a smile, just for him. And what passed behind his eyes could've been taken for none other than relief.

Whitty in the middle, they set off down Piccadilly.

"Do you know, Lady Tilly," said Whitty, a slight slur to his words, "that Lord Rhys here—I call him Ossie, by the way—is me oldest friend in the world?"

"Is that so?"

"Aye, it is." He was nodding a touch too adamantly for the maintenance of his balance. It was a good thing she and Rhys had hooked their arms through his on either side. "Thirteen years old at Eton." Now, his head was shaking from side to side. "A dead lonely age to toss a boy to the Arctic winds of boarding school. Oh, how I missed Nanny." He drew suddenly inward, then as suddenly brightened. "As you may have gathered by now, I'm a chap who likes a convivial gathering. None of this darkened-brow, romantic bosh for us. Am I right, Ossie?"

"Right you are, Whitty."

"Can't be arsed a whit for that rubbish. Why not just have fun? So, one night that first year, I reckoned I could sneak out of Hawtrey House and find my way to the nearest public house. And who did I meet at the gate at the end of the drive doing the exact same thing?" A boisterous guffaw sprang from his gut. "*This* waster," he said with great affection.

Rhys snorted.

His dimples gifted a glimpse of the daring boy he once was.

"Except," continued Whitty, "*this* waster had already been sneaking out every night for a fortnight." Again, came his jolly roll of laughter. "You see, at the age of thirteen, Rhys already stood at six feet and was the tallest boy in our year. *Me?*" He snorted wetly. "I was the same age and half his size. To look at us side by side, the hard of seeing could've taken us for father and son."

Rhys shook his head on a wry chuckle. "Didn't we try it once?"

Whitty's face brightened. "By gads, we did! And it worked."

"Until you edged up to the bartop and demanded a jigger of whisky with your glass of milk."

Both men roared with laughter, and Tilly couldn't help joining in.

It wasn't until Rhys guided them onto a quiet street that Whitty took note of his surroundings. His brow crinkled with befuddlement. "Ain't Brooks's the other way?"

"We're going to my flat on Bennet Street," said Rhys.

Tilly felt her eyebrows lift. That was news to her. Though she did like the idea of seeing how he lived.

Whitty's brow furrowed as he gave this surprising information a penetrative think. His brow, at last, released. "As long as there's whisky."

Rhys didn't miss a beat. "There will be tea."

Whitty's feet stuttered to a dead stop, pulling them all up with him. "*Tea?*" Whitty instantly looked twenty-five percent more sober.

Rhys nodded, firm. "Tea."

"What is this?" No mistaking the note of betrayal in Whitty's voice. "Is this a kidnapping?"

"Now, Whitty—"

"Don't *Now, Whitty* me."

"If you'll just see—"

Whitty gave a great, long shake, like a dog returned from a swim who was now expelling the water from his fur, in the process freeing himself from Tilly and Rhys's grasp. Then, liberated, he whirled around and started running until he reached the end of the street, his head frantically bobbing left and right at the apparent dead end before scuttling sideways into a narrow snicket and disappearing from view.

All the while, Tilly and Rhys stood rooted in place, watching Whitty's desperate progress, dumbstruck and gobsmacked.

"That was…" began Rhys, staring at the last place they'd seen Whitty.

"Unexpected?"

"I didn't know he could run that fast."

"While tight as a tick," said Tilly, nodding, impressed. "Imagine how fast he could go without half a bottle of whisky in him."

"Hard to, actually."

Like that, it struck Tilly.

She knew what tonight was all about.

"So, Whitty was your second noble deed, then."

Rhys nodded. "Was supposed to be." He shook his head. "I thought I could get him out of the clubs and have a quiet chat about the change in my life and the good it's done me."

Tilly understood. "And he would suddenly want that life for himself."

Rhys snorted. "Over tea."

A giggle escaped Tilly. "Tea might've been the feather that broke the horse's back."

Rhys's face turned serious. "I'm not giving up." He reached out and grabbed her hand. "Come on."

Next thing Tilly knew, her hand was clasped in his and she was dashing down the street alongside a Rhys as determined as she'd ever seen him as they followed Whitty's trail to the narrow confines of the snicket, then onto another street, soon finding themselves back on St. James's and facing the impressive Portland stone facade of Brooks's club.

Lawks, didn't it just look like an establishment for nobs.

Gasping for breath, Rhys faced her. "They won't let you in."

"Oh, the wretched lot of woman."

A smile twitched about his mouth, even as earnestness warmed his eyes. "You'll wait here?"

He wasn't telling.

He was asking.

And how she liked that.

"I'll be here."

His eyes searched hers one last time, then he nodded

and was off, taking the front steps two at a time. The doorman saw Rhys coming and had the door swung wide before he even reached the top step.

In case Tilly had any doubts that every door was open to a lord, here they were put to rest.

She pulled her black velvet, wool-lined cloak snug around her and crossed her arms over her chest, thankful for the woolen stockings she'd had the forethought to wear tonight.

However, she'd only just settled into the wait when the front door crashed open and out flew a wild-eyed Whitty. Instinctively, she lifted her hand in greeting, but it froze midway as he careened down the steps, took one look at her, emitted a strangled, "Can't be arsed a whit," and streaked straight past her.

A few seconds later, it was Rhys flying through the front door and down the steps. "Tilly," he shouted, eyes bright with pursuit, "which way did he go?"

She opened her mouth to reply, but all that tumbled out was a great wallop of laughter that once started was impossible to stop. So, she pointed down the street and managed not to double over with the giggles.

"Well, come on, then," he urged, grabbing her hand to follow.

But Tilly was finding it mighty difficult to keep up with both this laughter and her feet.

Rhys grumbled over his shoulder, "Can't you go any faster?"

"I don't think I can," she said, trying to keep up and failing. "You go ahead."

That got his attention.

His feet stuttered to a stop, and he faced her. "And leave you?"

"I'm the sort of gel who always comes through all right, haven't you noticed?"

Now she had his full attention, his silver-gray eyes searching hers. "I won't leave you, Tilly."

She wasn't sure if it was the words or the way he spoke them or the earnestness in his eyes as he spoke them or a combination of all three, but that instant, she was cured of her laughter.

In her entire life, only one other person had taken her hand and vowed not to leave her behind—Isabel.

And look how life had turned out since then.

Lawks.

Couldn't life get serious in the space between one heartbeat and the next?

She noticed her hand was still in his when he tugged it, and on they walked, fingers twined through each other's, side by side, in a way that could be called companionable.

"I'm sorry your friend lit out on you."

He gave a shrug. "Should've expected it."

"I reckon the reformation of a rake has to start from the inside."

"I reckon you're right," he said with a shake of the head. "Whitty can really run."

And together they laughed.

Ahead appeared a grand avenue of plane trees. "Is that St. James's Park?" she asked. Her bearings felt all scrambled.

"Aye," said Rhys. "Care for a midnight stroll in the park?"

"I rather think I would," she said, prim as a lady.

She liked the smile that pulled from him.

Down the avenue they ambled, deeper into the park. She hardly felt the chill of the night now, her arm woven through his. So still and quiet, it was. As if the rest of the world had fallen away and only they remained.

And the stray thought wandered into Tilly's mind that she might not mind so very much inhabiting that world.

A world of just her and Rhys.

Something fluttered from above and caught in her eyelash.

She blinked it away.

When it happened again, she realized it hadn't come from the trees, but from the sky above.

She tipped her head back and squinted up at the bare-branched canopy and she beheld it—*snow.*

"Oh!" she exclaimed, pure delight rippling through her. "Would you look at that?"

She released Rhys's hand and began spinning around slowly, her arms extended, her face turned up to the sky. The snowfall wasn't heavy and lacked the feel of permanence, fluttering and floating as if it were lighter than air and wouldn't deign to sully itself by touching earth. Surely, it would be vanished by morning. But now, trifling and feathery, it drifted around them as if it had not a care in the world. So silent...so...

Magical.

"Lord Rhys Osborne—"

"Rhys," he corrected.

"Did you know this about yourself?"

"What's that?"

"You've got this bit of magic that follows you around."

"*Me?*"

"Yes, *you.*"

He shook his head. "No, Tilly, you've got it mixed around. It's *you* who has the magic."

The breath caught in her lungs.

And this time she knew it was the words themselves *and* the way he spoke them *and* the look in his eyes as he spoke them that fizzed the champagne bubbles to life inside her.

Those words…

He believed them.

Of *her.*

"Rhys?"

"Yes?"

"Would you like to kiss me?" she asked.

"Would you like to be kissed?" he asked.

"Yes."

12

R hys had all the permission he needed.

He could kiss Tilly beneath this magical, snowy sky.

In this moment, and every moment since he'd kissed her, it was all he wanted.

Except something sat inside him at an odd angle—and he couldn't quite lay his finger on it.

It was located somewhere in those words...

Would you like to kiss me?

Her head tipped back, her soft lips parted, she reached up and caressed the side of his face, her hand warm through her kid gloves—and his misgivings fell away. He took her heart-shaped face in his hands and pressed his mouth to hers—warm and soft against the chill of night edged with sharpness.

During and after their kiss last night, he'd thought it and her perfect.

Now, as his tongue grazed across her bottom lip…his next breath inhaling her delicate sigh, it was confirmed.

He couldn't explain what precisely set it apart.

For this wasn't merely about kissing a beautiful woman.

Or merely about kissing a desirable woman.

Or merely about kissing a woman in the interest of progressing the kiss all the way to her bed.

Not *merely*, because he supposed it was those things, too, if he was being honest.

The perfection of last night's kiss and of this kiss lay deeper—and it held a mystery.

The sort of mystery a man could spend a lifetime exploring.

Without realizing, instinctively he'd walked her backwards until she was pressed against a tree. Every one of his senses felt lit alive.

Something else, too—*hunger*.

Of a sudden, he was ravenous for this woman.

Inquisitive hands slipped beneath his greatcoat, brushing across his chest, then his stomach. An appreciative laugh escaped her, and she shifted back a degree, meeting his eye, a little smile curving her mouth. "My, Lord Rhys, what muscles you have beneath your clothes."

Lower, her hands slipped—to his hard and ready cock. Her hand grazed across his hot length that threatened to spend at any moment.

He groaned.

And it wasn't just any groan, but long and rasped and animal…full of ache and desperation.

A year, it had been, since he'd had the touch of a woman.

But the desperation ran deeper.

Somehow, he'd gone his entire life without the touch of Tilly.

His mouth again claimed hers with a slow, deep kiss—and again she brushed curious fingers along his cock.

And again, he groaned.

She smiled against his mouth. "You like that, don't you?"

His eyes slid open. A vertical line formed on his brow.

There.

Again, it stole through him—the same sense of misgiving from when she'd asked, *"Would you like to kiss me?"*

A little nervous laugh escaped her. "It's been a while, but isn't that what men like?"

"What *men* like?" At last, he was able to grasp what was tickling at the back of his mind. "But Tilly?"

"Yeah?"

"What about what *you* like?"

She blinked.

And, at last, he understood how to proceed with her. "Last night…" he said, low. It was that desperation making his voice gravelly. "I seem to recall you liked *this*." He traced a finger lightly along the sensitive skin of her neck. "And if you liked that, then perhaps you'll like *this*." His mouth followed the trail of his finger along that creamy column, his other hand untying the closure of her cloak. "Do *you* like that, Tilly?" he murmured against her.

"Oh, yes," she exhaled, her head angling to grant him greater access.

Cloak fallen open, his gaze arrested on her décolletage. His mouth went dry. Oh, Tilly's glorious breasts. They were the stuff of myth, so perfect they were. His finger trailed down that deep valley, his mouth following. One practiced tug of her bodice, and there they were, nipples peaked beneath the gossamer muslin of her chemise. He licked, then sucked a hard pink nip into his mouth through the fabric, his tongue swirling around the nub that had gone as hard as a cherry pit, dragging a low moan from Tilly.

Full and heavy were these breasts of Tilly's. He had large hands, but they weren't nearly up to the task of containing her.

Then her breasts weren't enough.

He needed to taste other parts of her.

Desperation had him on his knees…meeting her gaze as he lifted her skirts…his eyes asking permission…her eyes granting it.

Perhaps it was that rake blood yet roaring through his veins.

Blood still het up from the feel of the dice in his hand… driving him…spurring him on…

That hot, wrong feel of vice ripping through him.

But he didn't think so.

In fact, he knew it wasn't.

It was Tilly.

And Tilly wasn't *wrong*.

She was everything that was *right*.

He shifted forward, ducking beneath her skirts, immediately surrounded by warmth and the scent of Tilly...the heady scent of her sex. Unable not to, he inhaled deeply, those elements of her rushing through him straight to his cock, which throbbed...which ached.

He lifted her leg and at the line where her wool stockings ended, he began a trail with his mouth and tongue along that sensitive skin. A tremor quaked through her, he could feel it—*the desire...the longing...the anticipation...the desperation...*

He touched his tongue to her.

She gasped—then melted against him.

Oh, she liked that.

He didn't have to ask.

Slowly, deliberately, as if he had all the time in the world, he slid his tongue along her slit and produced a most gratifying little mewl of pleasure and frustration from her.

His blood blazed into a conflagration—lit by this...lit by *her.*

He entered her with one finger, as his tongue concentrated on the sensitive nub of her sex. Her body was now beyond melted. It had gone molten, as his tongue flicked against her, his finger sliding in and out of her. What a sweet, delicate cunny Tilly had—slick and swollen with desire and need. And though she'd gone molten, he sensed the moment a specific tension entered her. Release had started teasing, and she'd begun reaching for it. He pushed his finger deeper, increasing the rhythm of his tongue. She was close...so close...

On a sharp gasp, the breath caught in her lungs, and she went tense. With few more flicks of his tongue, release seized her and she was crying out and her quim was pulsing against his mouth, around his finger, as he stayed with her through the end of her climax, his own breath gone ragged, the blood stirred in his veins. He angled back, releasing her leg and allowing her skirts to fall. Her breath was coming hard in evaporating white puffs, her eyes closed.

Oh, but she was a vision of molten, sated femininity.

And he wanted more of her.

Giving her pleasure—bringing her to release—satisfied one hunger within him only to awaken another.

Her eyes fluttered open and found his. "Do you want me to reciprocate?"

He wasn't sure what he'd been expecting her to say, but it wasn't that.

He pushed off the ground and came to his feet. "That was about *you*."

The words came at a price—the severe displeasure of his cock.

Her head canted, a smile curled one side of kiss-crushed lips he wanted nothing more than to taste again. "You were pretty good at being a rake, I reckon."

"I reckon I was."

She exhaled a nearly soundless laugh.

Except when he'd been a rake, he'd been more concentrated on how *he* felt than how his partner felt. Oh, he would leave her feeling good—better than good, in fact—but that was all surfaces, wasn't it?

What he'd done with Tilly was about places deeper than surfaces.

It wasn't about feeling in one way, but a multitude of ways.

A confusion of ways, if he was being honest.

He was opening his mouth to start in on all this when she said in a near whisper, utterly serious, "That was a first for me."

Rhys felt his brow furrow. She'd been with other men. He knew that. So, what had been *a first* about what they'd just done?

As if she could hear his thoughts, she said, "I've never —" Her gaze caught on a point over his shoulder. Her eyes narrowed. "Is that…?" Her eyes went wide. "*Whitty?*"

Rhys twisted around, his gaze searching the avenue beyond their little, magical copse of trees, when it landed on a figure staggering across the open pitch. He supposed it could be…

"Can't be arsed a whit!" the man shouted to no one in particular.

No disputing the fact.

It was Whitty, all right.

Rhys turned back to Tilly.

"I think we must go and help him," she said, the voice of reason.

Except Rhys didn't feel like being helpful or reasonable.

He wanted to stay right here with Tilly.

He wanted to talk about this confusion of feelings rioting through him.

But he'd begun the night with the intention of helping

Whitty and now he supposed it was his duty to see it through.

Right.

He turned back to Tilly to find her tying the laces of her cloak.

She looked almost entirely herself.

Almost.

Her lips were yet kiss-swollen…her eyes yet overbright from the pleasure that had washed through her…pleasure that would yet be rippling through her veins…

Pleasure he'd brought her.

"We should get him before he legs it again."

A smile curved her mouth, which his couldn't help joining.

Then they were on the move, and in the matter of a minute, they caught up to Whitty, who took one look at them and made to bolt—except, this time, his legs were in no mood to obey.

"Oh, Ossie," he said mournfully. "Why are you out to prosecute—" His face squinched in confusion. *"Prosecute…"* He held up a staying finger while he worked through the word he intended, then said, *"Pro-se-cute* me?"

Rhys took Whitty's meaning all the same. "I'm not persecuting you, old man."

"Then why are you chasing me all over town?" Whitty exclaimed.

"Because you keep running."

"And whose fault is that?"

For a drunken sot, Whitty had him there.

Rhys couldn't fault the logic.

"If you'll just come—"

"Wait a minute," said Whitty. "Have you found…*religion*, Ossie? Is that what this is all about?"

An interesting question, that.

For, in an instant, Rhys knew exactly what sort of religion he'd found—The Church of Tilly Birdwell.

And he'd become a devout member overnight.

Of course, he couldn't very well say that.

Whitty's eyes went wide as saucers, as if he'd heard it, anyway. "You have." He shook his head, in awe to the wonders this old world wrought. "Lord Rhys Osborne, reformed rake. Never thought I'd live to see it."

Rhys snorted. "Let's not get carried away."

He had yet plenty of unreformed parts of himself carrying on.

Like the unreformed part of himself that had pleasured Tilly's cunny and ached to do it again.

"All right now, Lord Whitty," said Tilly, taking a step forward, "we're going to catch our deaths out here. So, let's continue this conversation somewhere warm, shall we?"

Whitty's imploring brown eyes met Rhys's. "Back to White's, then?" They shifted to meet Tilly's. "Brooks's?"

"My flat," said Rhys.

Whitty groaned as he allowed Rhys and Tilly to each take an arm. "I thought you would say that. But, by gads, I'll not have a drop of tea."

As last stands went, Rhys had heard worse.

Three abreast, they tottered one step forward, then another. Though their progress weebled and wobbled and, at times, lurched and listed, half an hour later, they found themselves staggering up the steps to Rhys's first-floor flat on Bennet Street, then once inside, depositing Whitty onto the drawing room sofa.

"I'll just…" The rest of Whitty's intention dissolved into a long, deep snore.

Leaving Rhys all but alone with Tilly.

"Tilly," he began and stopped. His gaze narrowed. "You're shivering."

"Oh, it's noth—"

"And you're wet."

"It's only the snow melted. It'll dry."

But those last words were spoken to his back, for he was already on the move. "I'm having a hot bath poured for you."

"It's gone midnight," she protested.

But Rhys was determined.

Tilly was suffering.

All right, suffering might've been painting the lily, but she was uncomfortable.

And he wouldn't have that.

In his life as a rake, he'd made much hay from his attentiveness and gallantry toward the opposite sex.

It was a central tenet of the rules of the game, and he'd been a master.

But that attentiveness and gallantry had been hollow at its core.

It had a single end in mind.

But Tilly…

She wasn't a game.

And there was nothing hollow in his feelings for her.

13

LATER

Lord Rhys Osborne might've been down on his luck and a former wastrel and rake, but lest Tilly forget, he was still a lord and lived like one.

All it took was the little tinkle of a bell, and servants were pouring a hot, scrumptious, bubbly, lavender-scented bath at two in the morning.

He was the son of an earl, all right.

For someone like her, someone born with nothing, she supposed it could be something that set her against him. How she could dismiss him as another entitled, wastrel lord—even the third son of an earl was a lord, after all— and take a cool, dismissive view of him.

Except that wasn't Rhys, the person.

She reckoned he'd been all those things, once, but *entitled…wastrel…*that wasn't the man she saw.

Likely, she would never tell him this, but losing his pa's ring to that rotter Sir Felix might've been the making of him.

She almost regretted what she'd decided to do tonight —which was to return the ring to him. She didn't feel right keeping it any longer, so she'd brought it with her. By holding on to it, she was preventing him from making amends with his pa, and she wanted that for him. After all, it was nearly Christmas. What better gift between father and son than reconciliation?

There was just one thing…

It would mean she wouldn't be seeing Rhys anymore.

No longer would they have anything that bound them.

Except she *did* feel bound to him.

When had that happened?

Well, there was last night—*the kiss.*

And tonight…

Oh, that had been so much more than a kiss.

Her body was still alive with it, as if a lightning bolt had fizzed the champagne bubbles in her veins with electrical current.

But there were other ways she felt bound to him, too, beyond the physical.

Which had to be an illusion brought on by them electric champagne bubbles.

Lawks, what was she, a former strumpet and present lady's maid, to *him*, a lord?

A *tap-tap* sounded on the door, followed by a low, "All right in there?"

She had a choice.

She could say *yes*, that she would be out in a few minutes. Though she would encounter no small amount of protest from her luxuriating muscles in the event she attempted to remove them from this delicious heat and these lavender-scented bubbles. How did a lord have lavender-scented bubbles for the bath, anyway?

It would've been that rakish past of his, wouldn't it?

Better a question left unasked.

Which left her with that other option sitting in her palm.

She could say *yes* and… "Would you like to come in?"

A slow beat of time ticked past. He was thinking about it. Then… "I would."

The door opened on silent hinges, and there he was. His coat, cravat, scarf, gloves, and all the rest were gone, and he was down to his bare feet, trousers, and white linen shirt, splayed open in a V down his chest, revealing a dark fuzz of hair and…*muscles.*

Lawks.

What a sight this man made.

He padded across the marble floor, grabbing a short, three-legged stool along the way, which he placed beside the foot of the bathtub, and lowered, his large body surely testing the stool's mettle. "Are you enjoying your bath?"

"Aye," she said, swiping a palmful of bubbles and blowing them in his direction. "And Whitty? Is he all right?"

Rhys snorted. "He'll be snoozing until noon."

Tilly's laugh echoed through the bathroom, bouncing off black-and-white checkered marble, then she said, "I have an impertinent question for you."

Mischief sparked in his eyes. "My favorite sort."

"Where does all your blunt come from, anyway?"

"Ah." His smile turned sheepish. "Well, as a boy, I charmed a great-aunt no end." He spread his hands wide. "She left me everything."

All right, now she had another question—one equally impertinent. "Then why did you gamble your pa's ring?"

"You're not a gambler, Tilly. I'm not sure you would understand."

"Tell me."

The moment stretched long as he considered his response. "There's a feeling that lights a match in the blood the instant the wager is made. And the more precious the wager, the more intense the feeling. It's hard to understand it with my logical mind. That night, I was short ready funds, so I took the ring. I'd done it before with no harm. I thought history would repeat itself." A beat. "It didn't."

It was just that simple, his eyes said, and just that devastating.

"May I make an impertinent request of my own?"

She nodded her permission.

"A sentence you began in the park, after..." He didn't need to say *after* what. They both knew. "I'd like you to finish that sentence."

"Remind me?"

"You said that was a first for you. Then you said you said you'd never..."

Oh, *that* sentence.

A sentence begun when she was yet mindless with the pleasure he'd wrought upon her.

But his silver-gray eyes shone with openness and

honesty and she felt like she could tell this man—though he was the son of an earl—*anything*.

"Last night," she began, trying to arrange her thoughts in a straight line, "was the first *first*."

"You're going to have to explain."

"The kiss," she said. "I'd been kissed before."

He cocked his head. He was listening.

"But I'd never chosen a kiss. All my kisses—the ones from that other life—they'd been bought and paid for. Some were better than others, but in my whole life, I'd never kissed a man because I expressly wanted to by my free choice." An unaccountable surge of emotion charged through her. "Until I kissed you, I'd never done anything with a man because I truly wanted to."

Still, he listened.

"My own desire and the choice to act on it was a first. Then tonight..." A nervous little laugh escaped her. "You took my choice and desire and transformed it into something else—*pleasure*." She swallowed all that emotion provoked. "In my experience of the world, desire and pleasure were the domain of men. I had just been a pretty vessel for their snatching of it."

Rhys swallowed, his Adam's apple bobbing. He looked suddenly wretched, but said nothing.

"But *you*, Rhys, you're not like those men, are you?" She sat forward, her breasts bobbing heavily beneath the bubbles. "No man had ever put my pleasure above his own." She was speaking as earnestly as she ever had in her life. "Until *you*." She was now close enough to touch him. But she wouldn't. Not yet, at least. She had even more she wanted to say to this man. "You wrought a transformation inside me, Rhys. I'm not a vessel. I'm a woman who can have a desire and act on it. I'm allowed choice and pleasure."

Her words echoed through the room, but didn't fall away silently.

Instead, they expanded into the air between them.

"And me, Tilly?" The question emerged as a velvet scrape across his throat, his gaze refusing to release hers. "Do you desire me?"

"Aye."

"Then, Tilly, I'm yours to have."

And here was Tilly, presented with another choice by this man.

To have him or not.

The thing was, if she was going to lose him by morning, then where was the harm in having him first?

Her hand, warm and wet, reached out and caressed the side of his face. In a way, she didn't know how to do this—how to seduce a man—for the outcome of every sexual encounter she'd ever experienced had been a foregone conclusion. There'd been no mystery or intrigue to it.

But this, like everything with Rhys, was novel.

Her hand slid across his rough, unshaven cheek and around to the back of his head, her fingers weaving through those loose curls. She followed the movement with her body, coming half out of the bathtub to press her mouth to his. His lips were firm, but soft as they gave over and returned her kiss, his hand reaching up and cupping her face, gently, as if she were precious to him, his other hand sliding down and cupping a breast. He groaned into her mouth, and she swayed forward, giving him more access.

"Tilly, you'll fall out of the tub," he said, his chuckle whispering across her lips.

She found a laugh of her own joining his, at the situation, at herself, her eagerness, as she released him and shifted backwards in the tub, slightly weightless. She could feel the saucy smile on her mouth. "How can you join me in here if you don't take your clothes off first?"

He didn't hesitate. He slipped his shirt over his head in a swift, elegant sequence of movement that might've been showing off.

Then he stood.

The breath caught in her lungs.

Lawks, the sight of this man.

How did a woman ever get over it?

Those broad shoulders and chest fuzzed with black hair, leading the eye down the ridged muscles of his stomach...down to where those long, capable fingers of his were working the falls of his trousers.

Her mouth went dry.

Which was the only dry thing about her.

One button undone, then another...and another... then...

He was free.

She gasped.

Rhys chuckled, and her eyes startled up to meet his. "My cock tends to elicit that response."

"It's so..."

"*Big?*" he finished for her.

She swallowed and nodded. As he stepped out of his trousers, she shifted to one end of the tub to allow him inside with her. He planted his hands on each side and began to lower.

On instinct, she stopped him. She wanted to feel him. That muscled stomach…those thick thighs…that taut arse… his shaft.

Tentatively, her fingers feathered up its long, thick length. On instinct, she angled forward and touched her tongue to him.

He sucked in a sharp breath. "Tilly, you don't have to—"

Up the length of his hard, muscled body, she met his gaze. "Isn't this about what *I* want?"

"Aye." His voice had gone to velvet gravel.

"I want to feel you this way, Rhys."

She dragged her tongue up his shaft. How hot and smooth he was against her. Hard as iron, but so very human—strong and vulnerable.

His fingers twined through her hair as she took him into her mouth and used her hand for the other half that wouldn't fit. She swirled her tongue around the crown and moved on him.

This was pleasure not simply received, but pleasure freely given.

And, *oh*, how that distinction increased her desire— every moan…every groan…making him wild for her.

And, oh, how she liked him like this—*wild for her.*

"Tilly, I can't take much more," he uttered…*pleaded*… *begged*. "I'm about to spend."

Slowly, she pulled back, her mouth sliding off him, dragging a tortured groan from his parted lips. Again, she met his gaze up the length of his body. "Then spend, my lord."

And she took him in her mouth and used her hand until she felt him tensing and reaching for the place he'd taken her tonight—the ether of release. She slid her mouth off him just as, between one heartbeat and the next, he tensed, then he was shouting with climax.

His eyes slid open, and he lowered into the water, facing her. He reached out, cupped the back of her head, and brought her mouth to his. Long and deep, he kissed her, her body swaying forward, slick and soft and hot against his night-air cool skin. He reached for the soap and smoothed the lather over her breasts, washing where he'd spilled. Oh, the ache between her legs… It was near excruciating.

"Tilly, your breasts are perfection." He rinsed them, then angled forward to trail kisses across them…softly sucking…swirling his tongue around her taut nips. She was on the verge of release, only from this. But, *oh*, she wanted more…was nearly mindless with the need. "Rhys, I want you inside me."

He lifted his head and met her gaze, his pupils flared, the irises pushed to thin deep-gray rings. Then he did something unexpected. He stood. "Come with me to my bed, Tilly."

He stepped out of the tub and offered her his hand. She took it, then she was in his arms and he was carrying her into his bedroom, where he lowered her onto his square, canopied bed and followed with his large body, hovering above her. Eyes locked, their choices made, slowly...deliberately, he entered her.

As they made love, as they clung to one another with a ferocity bordering on desperation, it was as if they existed in some place outside of time. It was that magic Rhys carried inside him. It translated here, too, like a spell was being woven around her, layer by invisible layer. No less powerful for its imperceptibility to the eye. It was there, nonetheless, binding her to him all the same.

Desire.

He'd given her access to that.

Pleasure.

He'd given her access to that, as well.

And now, he was granting her access to something else...some other part of him—not just his body.

A place beyond desire...beyond pleasure... A deeper, more intimate place beyond where one body spoke to another. For what they were doing with their bodies was simply the key turning in the lock...the door opening. But what they found beyond and who they revealed themselves to be...that was the space they occupied now.

Two souls, entwined.

But it was so very of the body, too, wasn't it?

The pleasure his large shaft was delivering to and exacting from her cunny, relentless, as he penetrated her and poured pleasure through her. That feel of him, heavy on top of her... How very much she loved this feeling. Even the scent of him—*amber, citrus, Rhys*—amplified this pleasure.

How at one she felt with him.

This act had never been so.

She'd never had the slightest inkling it could be.

But this was Rhys.

Everything was possible with him.

His hot, ragged breath in her ear sent little sparks of lightning through her, and she moved her hips to take him deeper, as deep as she could. That feeling was beginning to build inside her—release taunting…teasing…making her reach for it. He threaded the fingers of one hand through hers as he relentlessly drove in and out of her, their joined movement becoming more frenzied…becoming almost an entirely animal act—*almost*.

With every stroke, he pushed her toward an edge. She sensed release beyond that boundary—and oblivion, too. Her breath caught in her lungs, and she hung suspended in a moment that felt so very fragile and so very fraught with uncertainty and so very necessary… Her body tipped over the edge and an explosion of light flared behind her eyes and she was crying out as she fell and flew, her quim pulsing its release, her soul freed from its physical form. Then he, too, was tipping over that brink and groaning his climax as his head arced back, exposing the vulnerable column of his throat, joining her in this exquisite ether they'd created together.

He collapsed down, but not fully onto her as he rolled onto his back, bringing her with him, so her head was nestled into the hollow of his shoulder. "Tilly, will you stay with me tonight?"

She nodded, knowing she shouldn't agree.

Knowing she had more sense than to agree.

But it was Rhys asking and somewhere along the way she'd lost all sense when it came to him.

He'd asked her to stay.

So, she would stay.

What she needed to say to him would keep until the light of a new day.

For now, she was in his arms.

Exactly where she wanted to be.

———

Rhys lay in his bed, one hand propped behind his head, and stared up at the ceiling, golden dawn light creeping in at the edges of the curtains.

The only part of him asleep was the arm Tilly's head was resting upon, as her lush body lay curled into his side, the in-and-out of her breath warm and soft against his chest.

The rest of him was wide awake.

Last night, a few hours ago, he'd had Tilly.

Or, he supposed, she'd had him.

I'm yours to have.

He was.

But the course that lay before him was one he hadn't ever charted, for here was a woman in his bed that he didn't want to see leave it.

Yet...what use did a woman like Tilly have for a man like him?

She was a woman with goals and ambitions.

She was a scholar of her profession.

Tilly was a woman who was going places.

The only meaningful thing he had to offer her was more of what they did last night.

Which, to be fair to himself, was not insignificant.

A dry chuckle escaped him, little humor in it.

Tilly stirred, and he froze. He didn't want her to wake. He wanted them to lie like so for, oh, another ten or so hours…or days…*months*. If he had his way, he'd never let this woman leave his bed.

"Rhys?" came her sleep-soft voice.

"Aye?" he uttered, low. Perhaps he could soothe her back into slumber.

"Do you have the time?" The question whispered across his fuzzed chest.

Barely suppressing a sigh, he reached toward the nightstand, fumbling around until his hand clamped around the small brass clock. He moved it close to his face and squinted. "Half past six."

Tilly bolted upright on a, *"Lawks,"* her heavy breasts bouncing.

Oh, lord, he couldn't look at her breasts.

He couldn't *not* look at her breasts.

His cock had certainly noticed and gone hard as iron.

"Half six?" She scrambled off the bed. "I have to get home or I'm going to look a right old harlot of Babylon."

Her movements both frantic and focused, she crossed the bedchamber to the hearth, where her clothes were draped over the fire screen to dry, and began dressing.

"Do you require assistance?"

Half of him hoped she would say *yes*; the other half understood a *no* would better further her goal of successfully clothing her body. For if he helped and put his hands on her, he wouldn't be able to keep those same hands off her.

So, he rolled out of bed, donned his robe, and went to stand beside the hearth. Offhand, he said, "I reckon I'll need to have another go at my second noble deed."

During the delivery of those words, Tilly had gone still.

"Not with Whitty, of course," he said on a dry laugh. "Though, I will try talking to him after he wakes. Might as well, I suppose. I've come this far." Another dry laugh.

Neither laugh had she reciprocated.

Which wasn't like Tilly.

She finished lacing her boots, then turned and met his gaze. "Well…"

She had something to say, it was clear—but she was having trouble saying it.

"Yes?"

The heavy footstep of foreboding crept through him.

He didn't like that look in her eye—*apologetic… determined.*

It was only when she dug into an interior pocket of her black velvet cloak that he realized she was fully, decidedly dressed.

She was ready to leave.

Her hand emerged holding something shiny.

Rhys blinked.

On her palm lay Papa's signet ring.

"Here," she said. She was offering it to him.

Rhys didn't move to take it. "What do you mean, *here*?"

"You can have it back."

"But I haven't earned it."

No, no, no.

If she gave him the ring now, then time was up.

Their time was up.

Carefully, she set the ring on the table nearest her, the embers from the fireplace imbuing the gold with a mellow shine, the cabochon emerald glowing an otherworldly green.

A thing of beauty and power, that ring—and Rhys wished she would keep it.

"Return it to your pa, Rhys, and make your amends."

"But the noble deeds—"

She didn't let him finish his protest. "You *are* noble, Rhys. In here." She tapped her chest directly above her heart. "You just need to believe it of yourself and let it guide you. I believe it of you."

And that was her case made.

Rhys watched, gobsmacked and gutted, as she gathered her cloak about her, then crossed the room to the door. It was only when her hand closed around the handle that she hesitated. She glanced over her shoulder, a war in her eyes. Then she released the handle and doubled back to stand before him.

"I have something else to say."

Rhys's heart throbbed and threatened to break free of his chest. His heart knew what words it hoped she would speak.

And he knew he would say them back to her.

"Thank you," she said.

His brow formed a deep trench in his forehead from which it might never recover. "*Thank you?*"

"Yes."

"You're *thanking* me?"

She nodded. "For last night and the night before, actually."

He was trying to get this straight, truly. But he was having a devil of a time... "You're thanking me for... *what?*... Tupping you?" He might feel a hair insulted.

A blush staining her cheeks, she shook her head. "I'm thanking you for introducing me to parts of myself that I didn't know existed."

"Like?" What was he hearing, anyway?

"Well, desire, for one. And pleasure, for another." The tips of her ears had gone red.

But Rhys had no interest in sparing her blushes. "And that's *all* I introduced you to?"

She blinked.

He shouldn't have said it, but those hopes of his had embedded deep into his heart, he now understood.

"Have a happy Christmas, Rhys."

And with that, she made her way to the door and, this time, through it.

She was gone.

He shoved to his feet and crossed the room, only stopping when he was within reaching distance of the ring. He lifted and held it to the meager light.

This ring had a lot to answer for.

It had first been the unmaking of him.

Then the making.

And now the unmaking again.

The loss of it had brought Tilly to him.

And now with the attainment of it, he'd lost her.

In truth, he felt piqued and slightly swindled.

In giving him the ring, Tilly had denied him more time with her.

Time, he realized now, he'd been counting on.

But what she'd done, he also saw, she'd done out of self-lessness—out of that good in her heart.

Return it to your pa, Rhys, and make your amends.

Really, there was but one word that fit this feeling inside him.

He wasn't feeling piqued or swindled.

Bereft.

That was the only word for this feeling channeling through and hollowing him out.

Utterly, completely, irretrievably *bereft*.

14

ASHBURN HALL, HAMPSHIRE,
THREE DAYS LATER

Rhys urged his horse through the familiar gargoyle-topped, wrought iron gate that opened onto the ancestral lands of the Earls of Ashburn.

He was home.

But as he made his way up the long gravel drive with stout oak trees to either side and onto Ashburn Hall's wide forecourt, it felt little like a homecoming.

"Lord Rhys," said Letlow, Ashburn's long-time butler, hurrying down the front steps, as Rhys dismounted and handed the reins to a lad, "we weren't expecting you until Christmas Eve."

The servants were all regarding him in the way they used to—doubtfully, as if he were likely too drunk to know that Christmas Eve was four days hence.

But Rhys wasn't drunk.

He hadn't had a drop, though he'd been properly tempted when Whitty had rolled off his sofa three days ago and pulled a flask from some inner pocket. When his friend had offered him a swig, Rhys had known no greater temptation in his entire life. After all, he'd been utterly bereft, and one drank whisky in utterly bereft times.

Who would've blamed him for taking a swig?

It was what one did.

Yet, somehow, Rhys had dug deep into inner reserves and resisted.

And he'd continued to resist in all the seconds… minutes…hours…and trio of days since.

So, now, he was able to look Letlow in the eye and say, soberly, "Is the earl about?"

The butler nodded. "Of course, Lord Rhys."

A few minutes later, Rhys was following Letlow into the study, where Papa stood before a large rectangular table with his estate manager, Landry. While his presence yet remained unregistered, Rhys felt remnants of childhood memory slip through him, brought on by the familiar scent of leather, books, and tobacco specific to this room. As a boy, of all the thirty or so rooms in Ashburn Hall, this one had been his favorite.

"Lord Rhys, milord," intoned Letlow.

Papa's head lifted. It wasn't a smile of welcome that greeted Rhys, but a subtle creasing of the brow.

Wariness.

And hadn't Rhys spent a dozen wastrel years earning that cool, wary smile from his father?

"Have I caught you at an inconvenient time?" he asked.

"Landry and I were just finishing up."

Rhys took a step forward. "What are those? Land surveys?"

"A neighboring baron has offered us the purchase of the fifty acres abutting our northern boundary. We're deciding on a fair offer."

Fairness—another memory from childhood.

Papa was immovable when it came to fairness. It was why his tenants respected him so.

Landry took his leave, and Papa indicated Rhys take a seat on the sofa beside the hearth, which roared with a lively fire. Papa settled into the leather wingback opposite and waited for Rhys to state his business. "Shall I ring for tea?"

"I'm not hungry."

"Perhaps a finger of whisky?"

"I haven't touched a drop in over a year."

Papa's brow lifted. "*Truly?*"

The question had been a test, Rhys understood that. "Truly."

"Jasper mentioned having seen you at White's."

Rhys supposed he should've expected Jasper to report back to Papa—and Rhys didn't blame his brother. Jasper would've wanted to brace Papa for the possibility—*probability*—that Rhys had slid back into old wastrel habits. It would've been motivated by the need to protect their father, and Rhys couldn't begrudge Jasper that.

"I've stayed the course," said Rhys.

Papa nodded, and Rhys noted a flash of relief behind his father's brown eyes.

In a strange way, Papa's relief hit him harder than his initial wariness had. For years, his third son had been a source of worry—he still was—for this parent who had never been anything other than kind and generous to him.

And what struck through Rhys was shame.

But, perhaps, today could be the first step on a new path forward.

Make your amends.

Tilly's words echoing through and propelling him, he dug into an interior coat pocket and retrieved the signet ring, which he placed on the low table between him and his father.

Papa's eyebrows winged together. "Is that—"

"It's your ring."

Papa reached for the ring and slid it onto his pinky. He squeezed his hand into a fist and released, testing its weight and feel.

"Papa," said Rhys, "I must offer my sincere apology for taking and losing it."

"You've already apologized, Rhys."

A hard note sounded in Papa's voice.

A hard note Rhys had spent years earning as he'd done as he liked and apologized later—over and over again.

"Did you earn it back the way you lost it?"

Again that hard note.

But the question was a fair one.

Rhys shook his head. "I didn't win it back. I had to earn it back."

"Earn it?"

"With noble deeds."

Papa considered Rhys for a long moment. "I'm afraid you'll have to explain."

Where to begin… "As you know," said Rhys, "I lost the ring in a card game."

"Loo, as I recall."

"Well, it took a year, but I managed to get into another game with the rotter who took it off me."

Head cocked, Papa was listening.

"Except," continued Rhys, "I didn't count on Tilly."

Papa's brow furrowed. "Who is Tilly?"

"She's the one who won the ring in that card game."

"So, you, in fact, lost the ring in a card game a second time."

"Aye."

Papa heaved a slightly exasperated sigh. "Then how did you get it from this Tilly person?"

This Tilly person.

A surge of defensiveness rose inside Rhys. "You can refer to her as Miss Birdwell."

Papa nodded, slowly, but held his silence.

"She would only let me earn the ring back with three noble deeds."

An incredulous laugh escaped Papa. "The cheek." None of his incredulity having faded, he shook his head. "Son, it's quite a life you live."

Rhys snorted. "For better and worse. Mostly worse, though." On second thought… "But Tilly is on the better side of the scale."

"So, she made you earn the ring."

"She did."

"Good woman."

"The best I've ever known."

How wretched Rhys sounded, even to his own ears.

From the way Papa's eyes narrowed, he'd caught that wretchedness. "And now?"

"Now *what?*"

"Now that you've returned the ring to me, what are your plans for the future?"

Future?

Rhys could barely get through one minute into the next. "I've never been all that skilled in thinking in those terms."

"And Miss Birdwell?" asked Papa. "Is she?"

Rhys blinked. "She is."

Papa considered Rhys for another long moment and seemed to make up his mind about something. "With the birth of my first son," he said, "I'd done my duty by the earldom and produced an heir. And when my second son came along, I knew the line to be completely secure. Then came my third son—*you*—and you were such a happy baby, then a charming child, and all anyone wanted to do was love and coddle you. Your mother and I gave you everything—and were happy to do so—except for one crucial thing. We didn't give you direction." Papa inhaled deeply and exhaled. "As the happy, charming, coddled person you were, you took all the easiest paths. And as most easy paths tend to flow downhill, there you went. By the time I noticed, your mother had passed, and it felt too late to intervene."

Rhys swallowed against the hard knot that had formed in his throat.

This wasn't easy to hear.

"And, son, that was where I failed you a second time."

Rhys had difficulty drawing breath.

"Can I ask you a question?"

"Aye."

"Now that you've recovered *this*"—Papa held up his hand, the emerald glowing with flickering firelight—"are you returning to your old ways?"

"Never," Rhys nearly growled. He might've been wretched and bereft, but he wouldn't return to the life of wastrel lord and rake.

Papa considered him for another long moment. "I see a change in you, son."

Son.

Lingering unworthiness crept through Rhys.

"Any change in me," he said, "is down to Tilly."

"Then why do you sound like that?"

"Like what?"

"Abject."

"My acquaintance with Tilly is at an end." Each word followed the one preceding it mechanically, as one spoke when delivering hard facts.

"Because you earned the ring back?"

Rhys nodded.

"You're in love with her, aren't you?"

"I…"

Rhys blinked.

This feeling of wretchedness…of abjectness…of pure, utter desolation… It had a source, didn't it?

And wasn't that source obvious?

Love.

Love for Tilly.

He was wretchedly, hopelessly in love with Tilly.

"Aye," he said, "I love her."

"And she inspired you to be a good person?"

"She did. She *does*."

That inspiration wasn't in the past.

It sparked through him in this very moment—and every moment he drew in a breath and exhaled.

That inspiration was in the present—*now*.

To be a good person.

To be a worthy person.

To be a son worthy of his father.

To be a man worthy of Tilly.

He shifted toward the edge of the sofa, imbued with a swift, sudden energy.

To be a man worthy of Tilly.

That was what he wanted.

It only took the turning of one second into the next for wanting to solidify into resolve.

He would spend the rest of his days being a man worthy of Tilly.

Those hopes in his heart.

The ones that were bruised and sore and *bereft*.

They lifted their voice with a demand.

That he fight for them.

That he fight for a future with Tilly.

"I see but one path forward for you, son," said Papa.

"Aye?"

"Earn *her*."

"Papa?"

"Yes?"

Though it mattered not how his father reacted to his next words, Rhys had to speak them. "Tilly isn't a lady in the aristocratic sense of the word."

In their world, this was a matter of supreme importance to many.

Papa nodded. "But she's the key to your future happiness and stability."

"She is."

"Then you have my blessing, son."

And though Rhys hadn't been seeking his father's permission or blessing, a deep-seated part of himself had craved it.

"In my four-and-sixty years," continued Papa, "I've come to understand a parent can only be as content as their least content child."

Rhys shot to his feet, spurred by sudden urgency. Three days of riding stood between him and London—and Tilly. He had much to do. "I must return to London immediately."

"I thought you might."

"I won't be back for Christmas."

"Do what you must, son, to secure your future and your happiness."

Rhys understood what he must do.

And what he was going to do wasn't a noble deed to win or earn Tilly.

It was simply to give her what her heart desired.

And if her heart desired to share that future with him, then it was her choice.

The point was Tilly was free to choose.

And if she chose not to share her future with him, then he would be wretched and bereft, but he would have given her something her heart truly desired.

And his heart would just have to find a way to make that outcome suffice.

15

CHRISTMAS DAY

This Christmas, Tilly decided, was a right lackluster affair.

And not for want of trying.

She'd done everything this year that she'd done in past years—changed out the greenery in the drawing room… hung the mistletoe…lit the Christmas candles…laid the Yule log last eve. Further, her gifts had been met with nothing less than delight by their recipients. There was Isabel wearing the delicate gold earbobs that perfectly complimented her late ma's locket she always wore… Lord Percival packing tobacco into the walnut pipe she'd found at Fribourg & Treyer… Lucy playing tug with her new spaniel puppy, Bonnie, who looked the sweetest thing wearing her silver-studded collar. Lucy had tied a big red bow to it, which Bonnie kept trying her best to paw off.

Later today, they would all make the journey across the duke's manse to the east wing to take part in Christmas festivities with the whole of Lord Percival's family, including his brother and wife, the Marquess and Marchioness of Exeter; their five boys, ranging in age from twenty-something to ten or so, and for whom, Tilly, of course, had gifts; and the Duke and Duchess of Arundel, who always gave Tilly a present. Last year, it had been the prettiest enameled hand mirror she'd ever seen.

It all should've combined to produce the atmosphere of holiday festivity and fun that she so loved.

But as she sat on the chair nearest the window for light, flipping through the book Isabel had given her on the culture of the Indian subcontinent—she reckoned she had been asking quite a lot of questions about the Royal Pavilion in Brighton—none of that usual delight accompanying the spark of discovery fired through her.

And she knew why.

Choice.

She'd made some choices that had landed her in this spot of despair.

Of course, the choice that had pushed it all into motion was that choice to have a little wild night at a masquerade ball.

Then it was one choice made after another—the choice to hold onto an earl's fancy signet ring and teach his son a few life lessons...the choice to kiss Rhys...the choice to make love with him...

And now, she was left with no choice but to miss him.

That was new.

Just as she'd never chosen a man before, she'd never missed one, either.

A knock sounded at the door, to which Tilly paid little mind.

"You may enter," said Isabel without looking up from Lucy and Bonnie.

Irwin entered, but a second set of footsteps had Tilly glancing over—and her heart heaving a great thump and tumbling over itself inside her chest.

She hadn't known a heart could do that.

But then, until a month ago, she hadn't known much about the heart.

Though she couldn't rightly say she knew much more about it now, except for one thing—it was terrible at communicating what it wanted, and then when it didn't get what it had secretly wanted all along, it became sore and achy and unable to enjoy anything.

But, now, upon seeing who was entering the drawing room behind Irwin, her heart made it abundantly clear that its true desire had arrived.

Rhys.

Oh, wasn't he a sight for a sore heart.

The room went completely still, even the puppy.

Black eyebrows winged into a scowl, Lord Percival lowered his pipe. "*Osborne?*" It was as if he refused to believe what his eyes were telling him. "As I told you, *I* would contact *you* when I have word about—"

Rhys shook his head, interrupting Lord Percival. "I obtained the ring."

What was that note in Rhys's voice? Was it…*resolve?*

"Then a letter would've sufficed if you're here to thank me," said Lord Percival, dismissive.

But Rhys had the look of a man who wouldn't be dismissed. "I'm not here to thank you."

That got a lift of the eyebrows from the room.

Tilly hardly noticed, for Rhys's silver-gray gaze had shifted and had caught hers and now refused to release it.

And like that, the world shrank down to two—*them*.

As if from a great distance, she heard Isabel say, "I suppose you're here to wish us a happy Christmas, then."

His voice a low, velvet rumble, he said, "Happy Christmas."

But Rhys wasn't saying it to the room.

He was saying it to Tilly.

"Osborne," said Lord Percival, plainly irked, "don't you have a family to be with today?"

"I do."

Still, he spoke solely to Tilly.

Her.

She was the one he wanted to be with today.

She couldn't breathe.

His eyes burned with an intensity she'd seen once—on their final night together.

He'd spent so much of his life in the role of wastrel and rake, but here he was himself.

He wasn't in a role.

He never had been with her.

"I have a gift for you," he said with an imploring note that struck straight through to her heart.

"Oh?"

"It's not here." Beside that pleading note ribboned another—*uncertainty.* "Will you come with me?"

"Yes."

She hadn't hesitated.

This *yes* felt different from any other *yes* she'd ever uttered in her life.

This *yes* wouldn't simply lead her from this room.

This *yes* would lead her into an altogether different future from the one she'd seen for herself five minutes ago.

Her heart, which she'd only recently become intimately acquainted with, knew it.

Yes.

And she took his hand.

YES.

The first *yes* in a series of *yes*es today—Rhys hoped.

But he wouldn't push his luck.

He would take this one *yes*—for now.

Nerves jittering through his veins, his heart in his throat, Rhys found himself to have suddenly become his least eloquent self as he and Tilly made their way through Lord Percival's residence and into the carriage. To her questions like, "How are you?" and "Where are we going?" he replied, "Good," and "You'll see," and let that serve for conversation.

What he wanted and how he needed to be were at direct odds with one another.

He wanted to be close to Tilly...to hold her and feel the soft weight of her body within the embrace of his...to be one with her.

But he couldn't entertain those thoughts, much less act upon them.

Not if he were to play fair and leave her with that which she'd only recently discovered and valued most—*choice*.

So, when they'd entered the carriage, he'd sat across from her and let her ask questions and watch him with that bewildered, curious look in her topaz-blue eyes.

"You're being very mysterious."

"I know."

He needed to keep his distance from her for now.

He thought—*hoped*—she would understand.

It wasn't long before the carriage was slowing to a stop. Christmas Day appeared to be the one day of the year there was no traffic in London. He glanced out the window and saw they'd reached their destination—Burlington Arcade.

Tilly, too, leaned forward to glance out the window. Her brow wrinkled ever so slightly, but she held her tongue until they'd alighted from the carriage. "I don't think any shops are open, if you were thinking to pick something up."

"Follow me, Miss Birdwell."

He was being enigmatic, but from the smile that tickled at the corner of her mouth, he thought she might like that.

Thirty or so seconds later, their echoing footsteps came to a stop in front of their destination—*Number 27*.

"Rhys?" came her questioning voice.

"Aye?"

"What's this about?"

And though she'd asked the question, there hung a near imperceptible thread of knowledge within.

Before them was the empty shop she'd pointed out that first afternoon.

He dug into the interior pocket of his great coat, then held up a key like a magician revealing his trick. "Would you do the honors, milady?"

Though her eyes sparkled with curiosity barely held at bay, she hesitated the slenderest of seconds, searching his gaze. Then she accepted the key and twisted it in the lock. A few seconds later, they were stepping into the empty shop. It wasn't a large space, but it didn't need to be for Tilly's purposes.

Rhys closed the door and propped a shoulder against it while he watched her slowly navigate the space. She'd gone quiet, and he wasn't sure what to make of a quiet Tilly. But when she turned and met his gaze from the middle of the floor, he knew she wasn't about to be silent for long.

"Rhys," she said, "what is this?"

"It's your Christmas gift, Tilly."

"I don't understand."

But he thought she did—and was too afraid to believe in what was so plainly apparent before her. She'd been disappointed by life—by men—before.

Well, not today and not him—*ever*.

"Do you remember the day we walked past this shop?" he asked.

"Aye."

"Do you remember what you said?"

"I'm not sure." A bemused laugh escaped her. "I had a multitude of things to say that day."

He smiled, and with that smile came a subtle release of tension and, perhaps, a budding of hope. "You said an entrepreneurial spirit could make something of it."

Her gaze locked fast onto his, she nodded.

"That entrepreneurial spirit is *you*, Tilly."

"But I…" A trace of panic skittered behind her eyes. "I'm not ready. I still have fifteen years."

"Your time is now," he said, firm, almost commanding. "You're ready."

"But *this*…" She indicated the shop around them. "I'll owe you for this."

"I have a solution for that."

"Oh?"

"Cut me in."

A vertical line appeared between her eyebrows. "*Cut you in?*"

"Let me be your business partner."

She blinked. "My *business partner?*"

Rhys steeled himself. He'd practiced this part—in front of a mirror. "The thing is, Tilly, before I met you, I never had a dream of my own. But I like your dream. I believe in your dream. And I would like to share in it." Before she could protest, he continued making his case, "You would be, undeniably, the talent in this enterprise, but I have certain qualities I can bring to the partnership."

She tipped her head to the side and crossed her arms over her chest. Was that a smile twitching about her mouth? "Such as?"

"Well, I was able to get us the lease on this shop."

"Fair play."

"And there's the *Lord* before my name," he said, honestly. "It will help."

It was simply the workings of this world, and they both knew it.

"And I have an undeniable charm that will work well with suppliers and such."

She eyed him up and down in slow appraisal. "You do have those dimples."

He would've smiled, but was too beset by nerves. The thought of her saying *no…*

No.

She wouldn't say *no.*

He wasn't above fighting dirty and using his dimples, either.

"Tilly," he said, "I know you don't want to rely on anyone, but wouldn't it be nice to have a partner?" Here was the heart of his case. "Someone with whom you can share your dream?" A beat. "*Me.*"

"Rhys," she said, suddenly earnest, "*why* did you do this?"

He needed to be careful here, for this shop was a gift in truth.

He expected nothing from her in return.

"If I say *why*," he began, "I don't want you to feel obligated to reciprocate."

"*Why,* Rhys?"

"Because I admire you. Because you deserve to start your dream *now*, not in fifteen years. Because I love you,

Tilly."

He left the *becauses* there.

For another *because* ached to be spoken.

Because I want to spend the rest of my life with you.

But he couldn't say that…*yet.*

And perhaps never.

He waited for his fate with the breath lodged in his lungs, with his heart attempting to pound free of his chest.

"Oh, you beautiful, generous, good-hearted man," she said, rushing across the distance separating them and straight into his arms.

And when they kissed, it was with all the desperation and longing of that which was lost, regained.

She angled back, her gaze lifted, unshed tears swimming in her eyes—no small amount of joy, too. "I love you, Rhys. But not because I have any choice in the matter."

"Who would choose a reformed rake, anyway?"

She shook her head. "Because you were etched into my heart long before I ever met you. Because you have so much goodness inside you. Because you're the only man for me. But, Rhys?" Uncertainty flashed behind her eyes.

"Aye?"

"Can we just go on like this for a while?"

He took her meaning. "For as long as you like, Tilly. Forever, if you like."

As long as he had her.

That was all that would ever matter.

And when he pressed his mouth to hers, melted her with his kiss, it was to seal that promise.

EPILOGUE

27 BURLINGTON ARCADE,
FOUR MONTHS LATER

These last four months had been the busiest months of Tilly's life.

Of course, they would've been, she reckoned.

Going from one life to another was no simple thing.

She'd done it before, of course—a few times—so it wasn't new.

And though leaving the life she'd built these last nine years had been hard, everyone was encouraging, especially Isabel. She'd been the first to congratulate Tilly when she and Rhys had delivered the news of their business partnership later that Christmas Day. It had also been Isabel's idea to have the shop ready by the start of the haut ton's season in April, declaring she would be Tilly's first client.

It had been an unceasing whirlwind since.

Her gaze lifted and landed on the lord across the shop. By her side every step of the way had been that man standing at the front window display carefully tilting a hat just so on the dress form.

Rhys.

When he'd said he would be her partner in this venture, he'd been entirely serious.

"See how the brim of the hat tips up on the left side?" she called out from where she stood arranging silk poppies in the Venetian-glass vase that had been her Christmas gift from the Duke and Duchess of Arundel. Upon hearing Tilly's news, the duchess had proclaimed she would be Tilly's second client.

Lawks.

Sometimes, she could pinch herself.

Rhys cocked his head, considering the hat. "Aye?"

"Could you tilt it to the right? Give it that saucy angle ladies like."

"Ah." He glanced up from his task, silver-gray eyes shining with humor. "Now what, my captain?"

Tilly looked around the shop. How changed it was from the empty, dust-riddled space of four short months ago. Now, it contained samplings of everything a woman could need to start her journey toward her best style, starting with basic fabric swatches to determine a lady's most flattering colors for dresses, hats, and even jewels, to the various shapes and styles of hats, to the styles of the gowns themselves. In turn, Tilly would work with various dressmakers, milliners, jewelers, hosiers, shoemakers, and every other sort of tradesperson related to ladies' fashion to ensure every woman she worked with walked out into the world her most fashionable self.

It was a different sort of business and held risks, but she believed in it.

And as much belief she had in her talents and skills, that man over there who was now oiling the front door's squeaky hinges—that man who had brought her dream from the lofty ether of possibility down to earth and into the realm of reality—he believed in them even more.

"Tilly?"

She snapped to. "Aye?"

"You're doing it again."

"What's that?"

"Worrying yourself." He pointed at her. "That little line has formed between your eyebrows."

As she rubbed the spot smooth, he crossed the room in a few long strides and wrapped her in his arms in a strong, bearish embrace. He'd taken to doing that at all hours of the day, whenever the mood struck him. It made her feet feel firm on the ground, and she loved it.

In fact, she'd loved spending these last four months with Rhys, day and night.

Oh, the nights with this reformed rake…

The nights were even better than the days when he left the reformed side of himself at the bedchamber door and became his unreformed self between the sheets.

Aye, the nights were even better than the days, as she spent most of them in the new townhouse he'd purchased on Half Moon Street.

"Everything is ready for tomorrow. See?" He spread his arms wide before pointing toward the window display. "That hat is tilted at precisely the correct angle."

A giggle bubbled up. He always brought out the

laughter in her. Yes, these last four months had been the busiest of her life—but they'd also been the happiest.

And all of it was down to Rhys.

She angled her face so she could nuzzle into his neck and kiss it and feel the vibrant, steady throb of his pulse beneath her lips.

How alive was Rhys.

And how she loved him.

By every external measure, tomorrow should be the best day of her life.

But she knew it would only be *one* of the best days of her life.

So far, the best day had been the day she'd met Rhys.

But tonight, she was hoping to change that.

For she had a question to put to him, and if he said *yes*, then this day would leap all the way to the top of every other day of her life as the very best.

No day would ever surpass it.

"Rhys?" she asked, the nerves creeping into her voice.

He angled back to meet her eye. He'd detected those nerves. "What is it, my love?"

My love.

He'd taken to calling her that.

And every time—*every time*—he said those words, they struck a chord within her that filled her with such emotion she was amazed one woman could hold it all.

She inhaled, steadying herself for what she would say, searching for the correct way to begin. But she couldn't find the correct words, so she began with the truest words, instead. "Ever since I can remember," she said, "I've had this little animal being that lives inside me."

He blinked. "Oh?"

He hadn't expected those words.

Well, neither had she.

It wasn't a perfect beginning, but it was the beginning she had. "And whenever I've found myself in a tight spot, that little animal being takes over and tells me to run. Never once was it wrong—until it encountered you."

"Is that so?" He looked balanced on the edge of amusement to one side and confusion to the other. "And now?"

If she was being honest... "Some days, it still wants me to run."

Even as a smile twitched about his mouth, his eyes turned serious. "Can't say I blame it."

"You see, there's this other part of me that came to life when I met you." Oh, the emotion that rushed forward. "A part of me that is only alive because of you. A part of me that lives solely *for* you."

"Tilly..."

Sudden tears sprang to her eyes. "And that very much frightens the little animal being inside me." She exhaled a steadying breath. "I think it always will, Rhys."

Understanding shone in his silver eyes. And something else, too—*acceptance*. "That's all right, my love."

"But, Rhys?" She had yet more to say. "Me and that little animal being have reached an understanding when it comes to you."

He waited.

"The part of me that lives solely for you is what makes my life worth living."

He caressed her cheek with the back of his knuckles. She swayed into his hand before catching it with her own, staying it. She must say the most important thing of all before she could give over.

"Rhys, I want us to spend our lives together—as partners...as friends...as lovers...as husband and wife." Those tears that had rushed forward threatened to fall. "I know you're not going to ask, so I will." She inhaled and steadied her voice, which wobbled anyway. "Will you marry me?"

He searched her eyes. "We can have all the other stuff without the husband and wife part, you know. I'm yours, whatever way you choose."

She shook her head. "From the beginning, there was never any choice, remember? It was only ever *us*."

"In that case..." He stepped back, separating from her. Then he dropped to one knee and reached into his pocket, his hand emerging holding a...

Her hand flew to her mouth. "Is that a ring?" Gold and green winked up at her. "An *emerald* ring?"

"Aye."

Of course.

Wasn't it an emerald ring that had brought them together?

"Have I yet thanked you for cheating my father's ring off Sir Felix and rescuing me, Tilly?"

"But you'd already rescued yourself, Rhys."

His dimples made their appearance. "Ah, but you rescued me from a life without *you*."

"But *I* proposed to *you*," she said through laughter that was now flowing like champagne bubbles as he slid the ring onto her finger. "How is it you had a ring ready?"

"Actually, I've had it for a while."

A suspicion formed in her mind. "How long?"

He came to his feet and took her into his arms. "I had it with me on Christmas Day, in case—"

And here was suspicion confirmed… "In case I asked you to marry me then."

"Aye."

"And you've carried it with you since?"

"Every day," he muttered against her lips. "Just in case you asked me to marry you."

He said things like that—*romantic things*.

In truth, they were the sort of romantic things a rake would say to get where he wanted with a woman.

She liked—*loved*—that this reformed rake said them, too, to get where he wanted with…

Her.

In his bed—*oh, yes…*

In his life…

In his heart…

Forever.

The End

THREE LESSONS IN SEDUCTION

SHADOWS & SILK BOOK ONE

SOFIE DARLING

Lesson One: Don't forget to tell your wife you're a spy...
An absentee husband is one thing, but a dead husband is too much for Lady Mariana Asquith to ignore. When she travels to Paris to search for the body of the wastrel who broke her heart, she finds him—alive at the Opera and still far too attractive for her comfort. But not everything is what it seems with her husband…
Lesson Two: Don't let your husband seduce you...
Nick has sacrificed everything to protect King and Country—including his marriage. But after ten years of staying away from the woman he loves, he can't quite make himself drive Mariana away. He longs to be done with the lies and spies—but there's one last job, with a seductive partner at his side….
Lesson Three: Whatever you do, don't fall in love— again.

As they work together to save the French government from powerful adversaries, Nick must teach his wife how to be a spy, starting with how to seduce a dangerous stranger. Mariana already has some experience with dangerous men thanks to Nick, and she has her own lessons to teach him—like how passion, love, and trust just might save the day.

1

Married: Persons chained or handcuffed together, in order to be conveyed to gaol, or on board the lighters for transportation, are in the cant language said to be married together.

—*A CLASSICAL DICTIONARY OF THE VULGAR TONGUE*, FRANCIS GROSE

PARIS, 12 SEPTEMBER 1824

Nick spotted her across the cavernous expanse of La Grande Salle, and the breath froze in his chest.

There would be trouble.

From his shadowed position inside the opera box opposite hers, he could easily pretend she was just another sophisticated Parisienne. After all, he couldn't see her face as she made conversation to her right.

Except he didn't need to see her face. Her profile, limned in the soft glow of gas lamps, was enough for the heavy thrum of recognition to flood him with both a dread and a thrill that had excited him from the first moment he'd laid eyes on her more than a decade ago.

Why was she in Paris?

As if in response to his unspoken question, she canted her head to the side and froze as if she sensed something unusual, or was it someone unusual? He stepped deeper into shadow. Her gaze shifted sideways and unerringly found the exact spot he'd occupied no more than a trio of seconds ago.

He resisted the urge to run frustrated hands through newly shorn hair. She might have caught a flash of him. He couldn't be sure.

Blast. Why was she here?

She was here for him.

The thought sank in, and horror unfolded within him. Deep down, he'd known this day would come—the day she would enter his shadowy world.

For one thing, he was missing, or was he dead? Or maybe he was on a trip to Italy. No one could say with certainty. And he preferred it that way until he discovered who had sent two men to attack him in his hotel suite a fortnight ago.

The woman was more than trouble. She was a threat to half-formed plans that were barely treading water as it was. Ignoring her presence in Paris wasn't an option. If she was here for him—and she was without a doubt—she would find him. She was that sort of woman. She didn't fade into the background when it was convenient for others that she do so.

In fact, she only responded by foregrounding herself further.

He must find a way to seize control of the situation before it spiraled away from him, as situations tended to do around her. If she'd caught a glimpse of him, perhaps he could use to his advantage the curiosity such a sighting would stir within her.

She must be handled.

Which ran him square into the second reason there would be trouble.

She was his wife.

If one person in Paris could best him, it was Mariana.

"*Ma chérie*," Mariana heard as if from a great distance. "To sit in La Grande Salle is a privilege and a joy. Settle and experience it. You have *les fourmis*."

"*Les fourmis?*" Mariana's French didn't extend beyond the schoolroom basics of *bonjours* and *adieus*.

"The ants. You sit like ants are crawling against your skin," explained Helene de Vivonne, her mother's dearest childhood friend. "I lived in London during *la Terreur*. Have you forgotten? Everything is rush-rush. Tick one item off your list, so you can complete the next. Posthaste, you English say. This is not the French way." The older woman pulled Mariana close. "Savor the night, *ma chérie*. London has nothing on Paris."

Possessed with the attention span of a butterfly, Helene released her hold on Mariana and turned to her other neighbor, leaving Mariana alone to take in the crowded room.

From the ornate ceiling frescoes illuminated by a magnificent cut-glass, ormolu chandelier, and the parquet floor cushioned by dense Persian carpets, to Society's glittering *monsieurs, madames,* and *mademoiselles* in between, La Grande Salle was nothing short of sumptuous, the sparkling epicenter of Parisian Society. Inside this spectacularly gilded room, one could forget Paris had been in shambles not so long ago. This room could tempt one into pretending that the Revolution had never happened, and that it was only a wicked night terror revealed to be without substance in the warm glow of morning sunshine.

It was within this world that her husband had spent the better part of the last decade.Oh, Nick…

She slipped the note from her reticule and fingered its newly worn edges. She'd looked at it so often these last three days, she could quote its contents from memory:

9 September 1824

To the most esteemed Lady Nicholas Asquith:

It is with great and solemn regret that we inform you that your husband, Lord Nicholas Asquith, younger son of the Marquess of Clare, is missing, presumed dead in the service of his King and Country. He was last seen in Paris on 30 August. Please accept our most profound and sincere condolences to you and your family.

UNABLE TO COMPREHEND THE SUBTLETIES CONTAINED within the note at once, Mariana had sprung into a course of action regarding its more concrete elements. Namely, she would hasten to Paris and find her estranged husband —either dead or alive.

First, she'd seen to the care of the twins. Her sister, Olivia, took Lavinia with few questions asked, and Geoffrey would remain at school in Westminster.

She couldn't get Geoffrey's solemn, intelligent, ten-year-old eyes out of her mind. He'd known that something was wrong. "Tell me again why you're leaving in such a hurry?" he asked as if she hadn't already explained herself twice.

"I'm visiting your father in Paris. It will be a holiday."

"You never visit Father in Paris." His head had cocked to the side. "Or take holidays, for that matter."

"There's a first time for everything," she'd said, bright and shrill.

Geoffrey's eyes had only narrowed.

Even so, he, like Lavinia, had agreed to post an express letter to Helene's Paris address every single day. With the possibility their world had been irrevocably turned upside-down looming over their heads, Mariana needed to know her children were safe while she searched for their father— their missing, presumed dead father.

Next, she'd rushed from London to Margate. There she'd used a combination of desperation and gold to convince a reluctant Captain Nylander to transport her across the Channel in his East Indiaman. He was set to sail to East Asia within hours, and a quick side trip to Calais would be nothing to him. From Calais, she'd hired a coach, paid the driver twice his usual fee, and rode on to Paris.

If Nick proved to be alive, she would leave him where she found him and return home.

For a decade now, they'd been living the perfect facsimile of a Society marriage where they saw each other at arranged times of year—Christmas, Easter, birthdays—for the benefit of Geoffrey and Lavinia. Not ten words passed between them a year, and the children likely never noticed. It was the sort of marriage not uncommon to their social set, and not at all the sort of marriage she'd envisioned when she'd fallen head over heels in love with him.

She gave her head a tiny, clearing shake. That dream had been crushed years ago, a lifetime really. A better use of her time would be to focus on the present. If Nick proved to be dead, she would transport his body to London. At the very least, she owed the twins their father's decent burial at home.

Familiar panic rose, and the ground beneath her feet threatened to crater and give way. She wasn't certain what lay below, but she suspected it was a bottomless abyss from which she would never claw her way out. Even though she saw him no more than every few months, a world without Nick in it was too much for her brain to comprehend.

It simply couldn't be, and it simply was not. A force, intangible and mysterious, connected her to Nick. She would sense his absence if he'd left this world for the next. Except...

What if she couldn't? And he was dead? The doubt crept in and threatened to split wide into the unfathomable chasm of her nightmares, but she refused to consider that outcome.

Hands clenched into fists at her sides, a steadying wave of determination steeled her. It simply couldn't be. It simply wasn't. She would find him and prove it—for the children, and, yes, for herself. She could admit that much.

The playful rap of a silk fan across her knuckles snapped her back into the present. Helene leaned in. "I take it the tall drink of Viking water is no longer in Paris?"

Mariana quashed a sigh. "He left soon after escorting me to Nick's hotel."

Helene shrugged a Gallic shoulder. "His loss," she said, returning her attention to her other neighbor.

Escorted all the way to Paris by the imposing Nylander—it was true the man resembled nothing other than a Viking in both bearing and temperament—Mariana's first order of business on her arrival yesterday had been to place herself on Helene's doorstep. Within the hour, Mariana and Nylander had followed Helene's directions to Nick's hotel in the Place Vendôme.

"I believe this is where we part ways," Mariana had said to Nylander, her tone purposeful and businesslike. "I'm not certain you needed to escort me *all* the way here."

She'd darted a covert glance at the captain. He was the sort of man who could give an unhappily, even happily, married woman ideas. Even though she was here for Nick, Mariana saw how easily she could pivot and pursue a different path. She could invite this gorgeous man into her suite of rooms. She didn't owe Nick fidelity, especially after what he'd done.

"Shall I escort you inside?" Nylander asked in a low rumble.

For a long moment, she met eyes the blue of a midsummer sky. "I think not."

"I shall be in Calais for a fortnight to have a few repairs done to the *Fortuyn*. Contact me at Le Blanc Navire if you need further assistance." Without another word, he pivoted and strode down the crowded sidewalk as casual passersby parted for him like the Red Sea.

Mariana found herself the lone occupant of Nick's set of rooms, which once picked apart inch by inch, yielded no clues as to his whereabouts or fate, an outcome at once wildly frustrating and oddly comforting. She didn't know he was alive, but she didn't know he was dead either.

The man was nowhere.

Mariana worried the note between her fingers. Over the last few days, its texture had become as soft and supple as cloth. Yet, she kept it close for a reason: this note defied all logic. It was impossible to square with the dissolute life Nick led in Paris. Although the note was unsigned, it had originated from the Foreign Office.

How in the course of largely *ceremonial consular duties*—Nick's words—did one become missing and presumed dead in the eyes of Whitehall? She intended to ask Nick if she found him… No, *when* she found him.

"Mariana?" came Helene's voice.

As Mariana turned to reply, the fine hairs on her arms stood on end, and she hesitated. Her eyes darted left, toward the source of the feeling, but she found no one she recognized.

Heart pounding, she whispered, "Helene, may I use your opera glass?"

Helene raised a single eyebrow and handed the object over.

Mariana held the glass to her eyes and…saw nothing useful. Her overwrought mind was playing tricks on her. A phantom husband was the stuff of novels full of whimsy and scandal, not the stuff of real life.

The glow of the theater's lights dimmed, and the roar of the assembled dulled to a low rumble. The ballet was set to begin. All eyes shifted their focus away from the drama of each other and toward the impending drama to be enacted on the stage.

All, except Mariana. She couldn't succumb to the sugar-coated fantasy of the ballet. In an effort to relax, she exhaled every last bit of breath in her lungs and inhaled a slow, steady stream of air. But it was to no avail. Her heart a relentless tattoo in her chest, the walls of the theater threatened to close in on her.

She shot to her feet. "Helene, I need some fresh air."

Without a care for the other woman's response, Mariana darted out of the dark box and into a bright, empty corridor. Finally, blessedly alone, the walls expanded, and a self-conscious smile pulled at her lips. She was in danger of becoming the sort of excitable woman who tested her patience within thirty seconds of conversation. It was no state in which to conduct one's life. A restorative visit to a museum would do her a bit of good. Perhaps the Museum of Natural History…

An inconspicuous door flew open, and a hand shot out, closing around her upper arm with the strength of a steel vise. A scream caught in her throat as she was dragged into a pitch-black room, the door snapping shut behind her. Her heart hammered in her chest as if it was trying to break free of her body, and her mind raced in time with its frenetic rhythm.

Before another scream could gather in her chest, a leather-gloved hand clamped over her mouth, and an arm reached across her torso, trapping her arms to her sides and pulling her tight against a solid, muscular chest. She struggled, twisted, wiggled, and stomped—everything she could think of to free herself. But nothing succeeded, and her breath continued coming hard and fast through her nose.

It wasn't until her body stilled in frustrated exhaustion that she inhaled and *smelled*. Located in the scent surrounding her were notes she recognized—notes specific to one man. It was the scent of—

"Can I trust you not to scream?"

It was the voice of a dead man.

One Night His Lady

Nell and the Runaway Duke

Tilly and the Unreformed Rake

ABOUT THE AUTHOR

Bestselling and award-winning author Sofie Darling's passion for historical romance began in middle school the moment she cracked open *Wuthering Heights* by Emily Bronte. An instant and enduring love affair was born.

Sofie spent much of her twenties raising two boys and reading every romance she could get her hands on. Once she realized she simply must write the books she loved, she finished her English degree and set pencil to paper. (Ticonderoga #2 is her quill of choice.)

When she's not writing heroes who make her swoon, Sofie enjoys a nice weekend hike, a visit to a crumbling medieval castle whenever she gets the chance, and a slightly codependent relationship with her beagle, Bosco. Visit her website.

A small press bound by the belief that every voice matters.

Sign up for our newsletter to learn about new releases and more.
https://oliver-heberbooks.com/subscribe/

Follow us on social media:

facebook.com/oliverheberbooks
instagram.com/oliverheberbooks
amazon.com/oliverheberbooks
youtube.com/@OliverHeberBooksPublisher